The Christmas Tin

by Roderick J. Robison

This is a work of fiction. All characters, events, places, names, businesses, and organizations were either derived from the author's imagination or are used fictitiously. Any resemblance to actual persons, living or dead, or actual e-vents, is purely coincidental.

Library of Congress Card Number: 2012920403

ISBN-13: 978-1479271498
ISBN-10: 1479271497

For Mom and Dad, who persevered during challenging times and always put us first.

And a special thanks to Paul Reinhardt, editor extraordinaire.

Prologue

December 24, 2000

It has been said that Christmas spirit—that wonderful euphoria that sweeps through us upon realization that Christmas is near—arrives at different times for different people. It might come when listening to a carol on the car radio during the ride to work, or perhaps when dropping change into a Salvation Army pot outside the local Walmart. For some, it comes with the holiday season's first shopping spree. Others might experience it when baking Christmas cookies. Some people are infused with Christmas spirit early on in the holiday season; for others it comes later.

Being one who cherishes the holidays, I am usually infused with Christmas spirit early on in the season. This year was an exception though. My job and an impending deadline saw to that. I just arrived home late last night after being out of the country on assignment for the past three weeks.

But I do have Christmas spirit now. It hit me this afternoon when we placed our Christmas tree in the living room. We would have put our tree up long before had it not been for my business travel.

The past year has been one of much separation from my

family; my employment has kept me too long abroad. Like any job, being a correspondent has its downside. I was away for weeks at a time. I wasn't there to see my son Paul in his first Christmas pageant. Nor was I there to help decorate the first batch of Christmas cookies. And I wasn't home to see the stream of holiday artwork my kids brought home in their backpacks. Our living room walls are adorned with paper angels, snowflakes, Santas and reindeer. The stairway railing to the second floor is bedecked with a red and green paper- chain garland.

I have missed so much. But I'm home now, and there's no place I'd rather be than here with my family. I plan to treasure every minute of it. On the plane trip home I searched my memory for Christmas stories that my kids—four-year-old Paul and ten-year-old Anna—might enjoy hearing over the holidays. Storytelling has always been a holiday tradition in our family.

I fear that television, with its preponderance of high-tech toy advertisements, and the many other distractions of today's information age take away from the true meaning of the holiday. Sure, in their Sunday school class both of my kids learned the story of how Christmas came to be nearly two thousand years ago. But to my way of thinking, today's commercialism of the holidays no doubt distracts them from the reason we celebrate the holiday. I wanted to tell my kids a *real* Christmas story—a story that conveys the true meaning of Christmas.

I considered Dickens, but they'd heard the story before. I wanted something that would be new to them. I was pondering this when Anna came in from the kitchen and took a seat beside me on the living room couch. She was carrying her most prized possession: an old Polaroid camera—the instant film pack-type that produces photographs at the click of a button. It had been in the bottom of my desk drawer. I had given it to her recently when I came across it in searching for something in the drawer. Anna's eyes grew wide as she took in the newly decorated tree, the lights reflecting in the ornaments. She snapped a picture of the tree and handed it to me with a smile.

"Very good, my budding photographer." My daughter seemed awed by the tree and the magic of the season. I watched as her eyes moved from the tree, to the wall decorations, to the bay window facing our front yard.

"It's snowing!" she exclaimed. And so it was. Outside, the season's first snowfall was blanketing our lawn.

"Just in time."

The two of us sat on the couch for some time staring out at the silent snowfall. Then Anna's attention shifted back to the bay windowsill. In particular, she was focused on the small tin box that rested on the windowsill. We placed the tin there each Christmas season.

It's not much to look at, just an old rectangular-shaped tin with a snap-on lid. It was handcrafted nearly a century ago. The hand-painted holly leaves and berries on the tin had faded long ago. The metal is tarnished, and there are a number of nicks and scratches on both the tin and the lid. Most people wouldn't give it a second look.

"Dad, what is that?" Anna asked, pointing at the tin.

"You've been placing it on the windowsill each Christmas for as long as I can remember."

This brought a smile to my face. In all of her ten years, she had never before inquired about the tin.

"It's a Christmas Tin."

"A Christmas Tin?"

"A tin for storing Christmas-related items," I clarified. "Christmas Tins were quite popular in years past."

"It doesn't look too *Christmas-like*."

"Take a closer look," I advised. I got up and retrieved the tin from the windowsill and placed it on the coffee table in front of the couch. Anna looked at it quizzically.

"Was it Grandma or Grandpa's?"

"No honey, it wasn't in the family. It was given to me by someone very special a long time ago…during a Christmas that I wasn't at all looking forward to."

Anna gasped. "There was a Christmas that *you* didn't look forward to?!" This coming from a father who strung Christmas lights on the house the day after Thanksgiving was surely astonishing to her.

"That's right," I confirmed. "It was a long time ago."

"That's *so* hard to believe."

"It's true though."

Anna shifted her focus back to the tin. "What's inside it Dad?"

"Gifts and mementos from past holidays," I answered. And it was at that moment that I knew the story I'd tell my kids this year. Here I had been racking my memory for a Christmas story, when the best one I knew was right in front of me. A *real* Christmas story. A story that I had never really shared with anyone before.

"Can I open it?"

"Yes, but first you need to hear the story behind the tin and the objects inside. Otherwise you will not grasp their true meaning and value. Trust me."

I had planned to tell to Anna about the Christmas Tin when she was older, but what better time than the present? My little girl was growing up so fast.

"Can you tell me now Dad?"

"You bet," I replied. "How about you go get us some hot cider from the kitchen first while I put another log in the fire-place."

A few minutes later Anna returned with two mugs of cider and took a seat beside me on the couch. The logs crackled in the fireplace. Anna looked up at me with expectant eyes. I leaned back, took a sip of hot cider and I drifted back over the years…

Chapter 1

December 5, 1968

The season's first snowflakes swept across the school grounds just after lunch. By last period the landscape of Beldon was blanketed in white. This I could see clearly from my fourth row seat in Miss Harding's math class. Not that I needed the distraction.

The incessant clamor of the dismissal bell pulled my thoughts back inside the classroom. The students in the rows closest to the corridor had already bolted out the doorway by the time I reached it. I was about to exit too when Mrs. Trott from the front office suddenly materialized in the doorway. She was a buxom woman; there was no way around her.

"Principal Wilkins would like to have a word with you in his office," she said matter-of-factly. "Follow me."

Mrs. Trott walked with an air of formality as I trailed behind her down the hallway, my eyes level with the grayish blue bun at the back of her head. Holiday artwork bedecked the hallway walls, but I took no notice of it.

A few moments later, Mrs. Trott cut right and walked into the front office. I reluctantly followed her in. She turned and pointed to the principal's office across the room. "Go right in," she prodded. "Principal Wilkins will be in shortly."

During my time at Coolidge Junior High I'd never before set foot in the principal's office, nor had I in all my years at elementary school. It was new territory. The door was open. I tentatively stepped inside.

There was an institutional feel to the space with its avocado walls and dark wainscoting. At the center of the room was a colossal oak desk, a swivel chair behind it. A small ladder-back wooden chair faced the desk. Several diplomas hung on the walls along with water color prints of fishing scenes.

The room had but one double-hung window. From it I watched my classmates cut across the schoolyard on their way home. I sat down in the small chair facing the desk. Minutes ticked by. The janitor came in and emptied the waste basket. Then, Mrs. Trott put her coat on, readied herself for the outdoors, and left. The clanging of a steam heating pipe underscored the silence.

"Good afternoon young man!" Principal Wilkins boomed.

I stood as the man entered the room. "Sit down," he instructed, motioning to the chair. His penetrating eyes bore into mine as I sat down.

Principal Wilkins was a thick-boned, crew-cut man. He looked more football coach than principal. He had the reputation of being a strict but honest, play-by-the–rules disciplinarian who ran the school with tight reins.

There was little that escaped the man. On top of his desk was a manila folder. My name was written on the tab: Jesse Maclean. Principal Wilkins picked up the folder and perused its contents. His eyebrows arched. "I believe this is your first visit to my office," he said, closing the folder.

"Yes sir."

"It appears you've been an exemplary student until this year," he began. "Your teachers indicate your work is not up to par, son. They are concerned about your grades. Pretty much all of them feel you're underperforming."

He read from the folder. "Lack of attention…Missing homework…Seems preoccupied and distant…Mind appears to be outside the classroom." There was no misconception in his words. I had always been a conscientious student until this year.

"Your grades are dropping like a lead sinker, Mr. Maclean. I'm concerned about you. It seems you've been in a downward slide since school began. I know you're bright," he went on. "There's no question there. Your grades from previous years prove it. Anything troubling you son?"

"…No-no sir," I lied.

"You sure about that?" The principal's eyebrows arched again.

"Yes sir."

"Your teachers are concerned about you Jesse, and that makes me concerned."

His words were more subtle now; the lines on his forehead softened. Intuition told me that underneath the formal veneer was a caring man who was genuinely concerned. Concerned and befuddled by my indifference toward school work. I stared down at my Converse high-tops.

"Well, you need to raise the bar, son, and snap to! It would be a shame for a boy of your intelligence to have to repeat this year."

"...Yes sir," I muttered, avoiding his eyes. "I'll try to do better."

"You do that. I'll be counting on it. That will be all for now. I'm hoping this will be the last time your presence will be requested here for this matter. Do I make myself clear?"

"Yes sir. Thank you sir."

The temperature had dropped considerably since morning. I zipped my jacket up as I exited the school building. The landscape of Beldon was altogether different than it had been at the start of the school day.

The Township of Beldon, Massachusetts is situated in a gentle valley, framed by the Berkshire Mountains. With the season's first snow the mountains are reborn. The gray barren hardwoods and vibrant evergreens contrast sharply with the canvas of brilliant white.

From the top step outside the Coolidge Junior High entrance, I had a clear view of the town common at the top of Main Street and the business district below: two banks, an A&P, a bakery, Fiske's Department Store, a Woolworth's, a movie theater, a Gulf station, three eateries, and a barber shop. All of it was framed by the Berkshire Mountains.

My route home took me across the town common, then down the sidewalk that paralleled Main Street through the business district. Thanksgiving had just barely passed, but, like many small

New England towns, Beldon was already imbued with holiday spirit. An evergreen garland stretched across the top of Main Street, and all of the downtown storefronts were festooned in holiday décor.

Fiske's Department Store, the largest of the town's retailers, was the most vibrantly decorated business on Main Street. A pine wreath with bright crimson bows hung on the entry door. The door was flanked on either side by a picture window. Behind one window was a Nativity scene. In the other window, an electric train meandered through a Santa's village.

Fiske's was a place that had something for everyone: toys, candy, tools, hardware, craft supplies, sporting goods, women's & men's apparel—you name it. In years past, the store's holiday décor always captured my attention. My friends and I would stare through the picture window as the train endlessly wound its way through the Santa's village. Today, I merely glanced at it as I trudged down Main Street.

I passed by Woolworth's and the movie theater, then headed south toward the mill district—four blocks of three-deckers, boarding houses, and mill worker cottages, set against a backdrop of imposing textile mills. The mills were a cluster of dark-bricked three and four-story buildings with colossal double-hung windows and bell towers that seemed to stand guard over the town. People said that when the mill bells chimed in unison during the boom years, they could be heard miles away.

The mills loomed into view at the edge of the business district, their dark smoke stacks a stark contrast against the new fallen snow on the Berkshire Mountains. Beldon had not been spared the plight of New England's textile industry, as evidenced by the vacant parking lots in front of the mills. The old mill buildings stood eerily quiet as I passed by.

In its heyday, Beldon was home to six mills. The first to close its doors was the Browningten Mill, back in 1959. Two more mills followed suit the next year, and a few more held out until 1965. The culprit: cheaper labor and material down south and overseas. Now just one mill remained open—the E.L. Whittier Textile Mill. And it was running with reduced shifts as it was.

Just past the mill district, I turned onto Church Street. A few minutes later the street paralleled the southern shore of Johnson Pond. I caught glimpses of ice through the breaks in the evergreens bordering the pond. The ice looked safe. My pulse raced. Pond hockey season was here! My friends and I had been checking the pond each day since late November. The last few days had been unusually frigid; the pond ice was finally thick enough. Black ice—the best ice of the season.

Come winter, there was nothing in the world I liked more than pond hockey. The guys and I lived for it. As I approached the pond, Larry, Jim, and Rob were sitting on rocks along the edge lacing up their skates.

"Hey Jesse," one of them yelled. "Get your skates!"

How I ached to join them! Nothing matched the excitement of the first skate of the season. Like many New England kids, hockey was my passion and what I lived for. Bobby Orr was second only to my father in hero worship.

"I'll be back in while," I yelled. "Need to deliver the papers."

"Your loss."

"I know."

"Make it quick!"

"I plan to!"

I ran the rest of the way home. There was a bundle of papers on the front stoop when I arrived. Atop the bundle was a yellow envelope. The envelope, I knew, meant one thing: an address for a new customer. A new customer meant more take-home pay, and if I was lucky, additional tip revenue.

Looking at the address however, I quickly dismissed the notion of additional tip revenue. Patrons of the Beldon Manor Nursing Home didn't tip. Still, the nursing home was on the downhill portion of my route. And I already had three customers there. Delivering to one more room wouldn't be a hardship.

After grabbing an apple, I loaded my canvas shoulder bag with papers, hopped on my Schwinn, and pedaled up Beech Street. It was a long hour later that I reached Beldon Manor Nursing Home, a colossal turn-of-the-century Gothic Revival style stone building. It dwarfed the homes in the surrounding residential neighborhood. The usual medicinal-antiseptic aroma permeated my senses as I entered the vestibule.

The nursing coordinator was at the front desk and gave me a smile as I approached. My predecessor had a habit of dumping the papers in the vestibule, whereas I preferred to deliver them to my customers' rooms. I think she was appreciative of that.

"I have a new customer today," I informed her, pulling the envelope from my shoulder bag. "Ardella Calder. Do you know what room she's in?"

The woman looked up from her paperwork. "Down the hall to the end. Room 12. It's the last one on the right"

"Thanks ma'am."

"You're welcome."

The on-duty nurse gave me an approving nod as I passed by the nursing station. And a few patrons in the sitting room glanced up from the blaring Zenith as I passed by, making my way down the dimly lit hallway. All of my customers were on the first floor.

The first stop was Mr. Harden in Room 3. His door was slightly ajar. I could just make him out. He was lying in bed, an oxygen tank resting at his side. The man was in a deep slumber, the covers pulled up over his frail chest. I placed the paper on his night table alongside an old framed photograph of a young soldier in a World War I uniform.

Across the hall resided Ms. Kleiden, a ninety year-old woman who called me by a different name each time she saw me. She was in her rocking chair, an afghan across her lap when I arrived with her paper. "Hello there, Theodore," she crooned. "Been down to the river today?"

"No ma'am," I told her. There was no river in Beldon.

"Well, you be sure to bring me some more of those trout next time you go."

"Will do," I told her. I had tried to correct her at first, when the route was still new to me. But it seemed to fluster her. I would tell her my name, but it was to no avail. Then a nurse pulled me aside one day and intimated that it was best just to let her choose her own names and go along with it. She said it was more comfortable for the woman that way. So that's what I did.

"And give your little brother a hug for me," Ms. Kleiden said as I handed her a paper.

"I'll do that, Ms. Kleiden." I was an only child.

After that delivery, I made my way down the hall to Mr. Kuyer's room. The nurse assistant was just replacing his bedpan. Like Mr. Harden, he was frail and on oxygen— didn't have a lot of life left in him. He was awake though. He stood there stooped over in his bathrobe, his eyelids rimmed in red. His eyes were cataract-ridden, and it took a few moments for him to acknowledge my presence. Then he feebly reached his hand out for his paper.

"Here you are Mr. Kuyer. Good to see you."

"Eh?"

"Good to see you. I'll see you again tomorrow," I said, raising my voice a few decibels. The man accepted the paper with trembling hands, a smile etched on his face.

I went back out in the hallway and continued to the end. I knocked tentatively on the door to Room 12. Surprisingly, there was a reply: "I'm coming."

A few seconds later the door opened and there stood a woman I immediately pegged as a visitor, even though she was elderly. She was clad in dress clothes. She wore a woolen green plaid skirt and a red silk blouse with a Christmas tree pendant.

"You must be my paper boy!" she said triumphantly. "Come in, come in."

It was a first. I was taken aback. The lines on her face and the wrinkled skin bespoke her age—but she had the spunk and energy of someone much younger, though she walked slowly and with a limp.

"Here you go, Mrs. Calder."

"Please, call me Ardella."

"Okay Mrs. Cal—er, Ardella," I said, handing her a paper.

"And what might your name be?"

"Jesse ma'am. Jesse Maclean."

"Well Jesse Maclean, it's nice to meet you. Now how much do I owe you?"

"Nothing today. Collection day is tomorrow."

"Well, you be sure to let me know what I owe when I see you tomorrow."

"Will do…Ardella."

She smiled, and I was struck by the whiteness of her teeth and the youthful look in her blue eyes. I could tell she had been beautiful in her younger days. Still was.

From a quick glance around the room, it was apparent that her furnishings were altogether different from those in the other rooms. There was a strip of white linen over the top of the bureau, and a bowl of cinnamon-scented potpourri was centered on her nightstand. Pressed dresses and other garments hung neatly in the small closet. On the wall shelves were porcelain figurines and several photographs in pinewood frames. On the floor near the room's only window, there was a cardboard box of Christmas decorations.

Ardella caught me looking at the box.

"Are you as fond of the holidays as I am?" she asked.

"I haven't given much thought to the holidays this year."

"No?" Ardella studied my face. "Well, I'll have my decorations unpacked when you stop by tomorrow. You just might become infused with some holiday spirit.

"Thanks ma'am—Ardella." I doubted it.

"Thanks for the paper, Jesse Maclean. Good meeting you."

"You too." If it were any other year, her enthusiasm for the holidays would have been downright contagious. I pedaled back to the house in record time and changed into my hockey gear—shin pads, sweat pants, wool socks, a turtleneck, an old wool sweater and jacket. Then I retrieved my stick, gloves and skates from the closet and tore off for the pond.

Larry, Jim, and Rob were playing two against one when I arrived. The ice was pristine.

"You and me today," Larry called.

"You got it!"

Rob and Jim frowned. They were good athletes, better than Larry and me at some sports, in fact. But hockey was *our* sport.

I dropped my gear and sat down on a rock at the shoreline. My adrenalin was surging as I removed my right boot and loosened my skate laces. I couldn't get out on the ice fast enough!

I still vividly recall the exhilaration I felt as I began to pull the skate on…and the disappointment that surged through me when it became apparent that the skate no longer fit my foot. My skates were a size too small. Here I was at last, on what would surely be one of the best skating days of the season, and all I could do was watch. My skates—an old pair of Hyde Redlines—fit fine the previous season. That they wouldn't fit this season had never crossed my mind. Until now.

"Let's go," Larry shouted, banging his stick blade on the ice. "You got a knot in your lace or something?"

"Worse," I said. "My skates don't fit." How I envied the three of them.

"You're kidding!?"

"Wish I was."

"Tough break."

I sighed. "Yeah."

"See ya tomorrow."

"Later."

The three of them went back to their game as I gathered up my gear and headed home. On Saturday morning, after my paper route, I would bike across town to the thrift store and pick up a pair of used skates. It was the only day the store was open. Saturday was two days away. An eternity.

Chapter 2

The incessant clatter of power looms still reverberated in Frank Beauvier's ears long after punching out at the E.L. Whittier Textile Mill. A first-shift foreman, his weekdays were spent in the humid, cotton fiber filled air of the weaving room. The fifty-seven year-old had made a career of working in New England mills since migrating from Canada in his early twenties. He had held jobs in Lewiston, Maine; Pawtucket, Rhode Island; and Dover, New Hampshire, before moving to western Massachusetts. With the mill closures, his was a dying profession. But at fifty-seven, it was the only one he knew.

At six-foot-two, Frank Beauvier was an imposing man with dark expressive brows, jet-black hair, and a square jaw. He was sitting at our kitchen table sipping black coffee when I arrived home that afternoon.

*****

My father's employment as foreman at the Seasons Construction Company had always provided for us in the past. We were a small family, just the three of us, my parents and I. We never had much money, but Dad's salary had always covered the mortgage, taxes, food and other expenses… until his National Guard unit was deployed to Vietnam back in July. He'd entered the reserves part-time nine years before, during peace time. None of us ever imagined that his unit would actually be deployed overseas.

Dad's military pay was significantly less than his civilian pay; it didn't cover the mortgage, let alone other bills and expenses. With the reduction in income, Mom and I were in dire straits for a while. Then Mom found employment as a nursing assistant at the county hospital. And I found a paper route. Things were still tight though, so we decided to rent out one of the two bedrooms in our home—my room. Our home was a former mill worker cottage: a two-bedroom bungalow with a small three-season porch.

My mother and I spent the better part of August converting the three-season porch into a bedroom. We learned about insulation, weatherproofing windows, and laying carpet. I moved into my *new* room just before the start of school in September. It was spartan, with its space heater and exposed insulation stapled between the studs, but it was livable. Mr. Beauvier moved into my old room the second week of September.

Mr. Beauvier ate well balanced meals, and Mom received the security of knowing there was an adult home with me in case of an emergency.

A lifelong bachelor, Frank Beauvier was a man of few words outside the workplace. At first I tried to initiate conversation with him during our dinners at the kitchen table, but it was as if he'd expended all of his energy down at the mill and was keeping what little remained of it for the next shift. So it was that we slipped into a monotonous routine of sitting across the table from each other every night, communicating through gestures and monosyllables when it was necessary to pass a dish.

After dinner and dish duty that night, I retreated to the living room and tuned the Zenith to the Bruins game. The B's were playing Montreal. Mr. Beauvier came in just after the start of first period. He sat in Dad's easy chair. And it irked me.

"Should be a close game tonight," he mumbled—something the man obviously heard in the break room at the mill that day. Mr. Beauvier didn't exactly come across as the sports fan type. The statement was accurate though.

Phil Esposito scored two goals against his younger brother, Tony. The game ended in a 2-2 tie. I headed to my room afterward and turned in for the night without having completed any homework. Again.

Chapter 3

The following day, school was basically a repeat of the day before, minus the trip to the principal's office. Principal Wilkins did give me a look in the hallway that afternoon though. It was as if he *knew* I hadn't handed in my math homework. Maybe he did know.

"See you on the pond?" Larry asked on the way home.

"Not today," I sighed. "Still need skates."

"Oh yeah. So when are you getting them?"

"Tomorrow. The thrift store is only open Saturdays."

"That's right," said Larry. "I've got to help my father with some stuff in the morning but I'll be at the pond in the afternoon."

"See you then."

"Later."

The paper deliveries were relatively uneventful that afternoon. The dog that usually chased me down Pegan Lane was leashed to a yard stake; it could only bare its teeth and snarl. There were no near-miss collisions with oncoming traffic at the top of Beech Street, and I didn't slip on any patches of black ice like the week before.

When I reached Beldon Manor Nursing Home, the nursing coordinator was on the phone at the front desk. She looked up and gave me a smile as I passed by. Mr. Harden and Ms. Kleiden were asleep when I arrived, and Mr. Kuyer was down at the nursing station. I left the Friday edition of *The Berkshire Times* on their nightstands and picked up the payment envelopes they had left.

Back in the hallway I could hear Christmas music. It was faint, but grew more audible as I made my way down to Ardella'a room. Her door was open. Peering inside I saw that her room had been transformed from the day before.

Atop the bureau was a miniature nativity scene— to each side a red candle in a brass holder (which to Ardella's dismay, she was not allowed to light per nursing home rules). A half dozen white ceramic angels rested on the nightstand; the bed was covered with a holiday afghan.

Ardella's back was toward me when I arrived. She was attempting to tack a tinsel garland around the window. *Deck The Halls* was softly emanating from a transistor radio, and she was humming the lyrics. I knocked tentatively and she turned around, two tacks clenched in her pearly white teeth.

"Oh Jesse," she mumbled. "I'm glad you're here. Could you give me a hand with this garland? I'm just not as dexterous as I once was thanks to this bum hip of mine."

I stepped into the room. "Sure." I had time. She was my last customer. The only thing I had waiting for me was dinner with Mr. Beauvier.

"Excellent," she said, handing me the garland and tacks. "If you could drape this above the window there."

I was tall for my age. My mother said I got my height from Dad's side of the family—all of the Maclean men were big. I could just reach above the top of the window.

"How lucky for me to have such a tall paperboy—and a handsome one at that," Ardella beamed.

Ardella talked as I tacked the garland around the window. And she asked questions. She wanted to know about school and my family. And she asked about *me*. The woman was genuinely curious. She was also very upbeat and easy to talk to. None of my customers had ever taken an interest in me the way she did that afternoon.

I didn't open up too much at first. Perhaps the long silences at dinner with Mr. Beauvier had changed me, I don't know. But before I knew it she had me talking.

I told her about Dad being stationed in Vietnam and how Mom was working nights at the hospital. I told her about Mr. Beauvier too, and a little about school. I didn't dwell on my grades though.

"What are you getting your mother for Christmas?" Ardella inquired.

I paused for a moment. Unlike other years, I hadn't actually given it any thought.

"I'm not sure. There's not going to be much money this Christmas."

"The best gifts are the ones that aren't store-bought," she

stated. I didn't quite know what to make of that.

Ardella told me a little about her life. I learned she was born and raised in Virginia, had just sold her house down in Sheffield, and planned to move to Connecticut to live with her son and his family. She had fallen and broken her hip recently when moving some boxes. After a brief stay in the hospital her insurance company deemed it less expensive for her to recover in a nursing home rather than a hospital bed. She hoped to move to Connecticut by Christmas.

The phone rang a while later and from the conversation I surmised it was her son in Connecticut. My eyes drifted around the room as she talked and I saw that the cardboard box of Christmas decorations was nearly empty. The only item remaining at the bottom of the box was an old tin. It was rectangular in shape and had a snap-on lid. Painted on the lid were faded green holly leaves and faint red berries.

Ardella apparently saw me looking at it. "That's my Christmas Tin," she said as she hung up the phone.

"A *Christmas Tin*?"

"Yes. It's where I keep my most treasured Christmas gifts and mementos," she said. "From some of my most memorable Christmases. You'd be doing me a favour if you could place it over there on the windowsill, underneath the garland."

I reached into the box and extracted the tin. I grew curious about the contents inside it as I placed it on the windowsill.

"So what are the items inside the tin, if you don't mind me asking?"

Ardella hesitated. And a thoughtful look creased her face.

"They're likely not what you think. They are not store-bought gifts."

Just then came a knock on the door. "That would be my dinner," Ardella announced. "When we have more time, perhaps I'll tell you about the items in the tin."

"I've got some time tomorrow morning," I told her. The thrift store didn't open till noon.

She smiled. "Tomorrow morning it will be. I'll see you then."

"Goodnight Ardella."

"And to you, Jesse."

*****

When I got home I went to the kitchen and retrieved the coffee can that was secreted in the back corner of the cabinet above the sink. I placed my weekly earnings in it. As I returned the can to its hiding place, I heard footsteps behind me.

"Helpin' your mum out, huh?" For a big guy, Mr. Beauvier sure had a silent approach.

"Yes sir," I returned.

"Mmmhmm," he mumbled as he made his way over to the stove to heat up the supper Mom had left for us. That was the extent of our dinner conversation that evening.

Chapter 4

Sergeant Jack Maclean listened intently inside the fire-base's CP (Command Post) as the Lieutenant briefed them on the night's mission. Jack and three other men were to set up a listening post three klicks northeast of the company's perimeter. They would move out at dusk and spend the night listening for signs of enemy activity, then report back to the CP in the morning. The remote firebase had been home to Jack and the other members of his platoon for the past three months.

After the briefing, Jack walked outside, his blue eyes squinting against the afternoon sun. He passed the helicopter pad, the howitzer platform and the mess tent before reaching his hooch. Ducking under the flap, he made his way over to his cot. If he was lucky, he might catch a few hours of shuteye before moving out.

Jack removed his helmet and lay down on the cot. He pulled the picture of his wife and boy from his wallet. Bud Stiles came in under the flap just then and saw Jack staring at the picture. Nothing new there.

Stiles, Jack knew, was there hoping to trade chocolate for Jack's C- Ration cigarettes. Jack was a nonsmoker.

Stiles stole a glance at the photo. "You're a lucky man," he said.

Jack smiled. "That I am."

Chapter 5

The thermometer hovered at twenty-two degrees at 6:45AM Saturday. I could see my breath in the air when I went out to pick up the bundle of papers. It was only a few degrees warmer when I left the house a half-hour later to deliver the papers. The cold cut through me as I pedaled up Beech Street. The return trip downhill wasn't much better.

Mom was still sleeping when I got back to the house to pack the canvas paper bag for the second half of the route. She had worked another night shift. I did my best not to wake her as I boiled milk for hot chocolate.

It's amazing what a short reprieve from the cold can do. I was rejuvenated when I left the house for the second leg. The sun had removed some of the bite from the cold now, and the wind was settling down. The rest of the route had to be more tolerable.

Ardella wasn't in her room when I arrived at Beldon Manor. I would have missed her had it not been for the nurse on duty.

"She's in the sitting room," the woman informed me.

When I reached the sitting room, Ardella was standing behind a walker, staring up at ten-foot tall Christmas tree.

"Oh, hi there, Jesse."

"Ma'am—er, Ardella."

"It's beautiful, isn't?" she beamed.

"Yes. It is."

"It's a Douglas fir. From Nova Scotia. We're going to let the branches fall into place and later on I'll muster up a decorating party."

"Sounds like fun."

"You can join us if you like," she offered. "We could sure use someone with your height for the upper branches."

"Sorry," I said. "I'm playing hockey this afternoon."

"Oh, well good for you!"

"… I've got a little time this morning if you still have time to talk about the items in the Christmas Tin."

Ardella beamed. "That I do. Time is something I seem to have plenty of around here."

"Jesse and I are going to go to the cafeteria," she informed the aide standing nearby. "Could I possibly impose on you to bring us a tea and a hot chocolate?"

"I'll be in shortly," the aide replied warmly. "You be careful now. And go slow."

Ardella pushed the walker before her and we began a slow walk. "I was bedridden until fairly recently," she said. "But I'm on the mend now. This week it's a walker, next week it'll be crutches. And God willing, I'll be in Connecticut with my son and his family by Christmas."

The cafeteria was about the size of the lunchroom at school. The chairs were much wider though, and the tables were round rather than rectangular. And there was amber-colored carpet rather than linoleum. On the far side of the room, large burgundy drapes framed expansive picture windows that overlooked a small pond and the walking trail that encircled it.

Holiday music softly emanated from the ceiling speakers. Ardella placed her walker aside and eased into a chair at the table closest to the entrance. Then she said, "Jesse, could you be so kind as to go to my room and get the Christmas Tin?"

"Sure. Be right back."

When I arrived with the tin a few minutes later, there was a steaming cup of hot cocoa on the table. Ardella was sipping tea.

"Thanks for the hot cocoa," I said, gently pushing the Christmas Tin across the table to her.

"Thank *you*," Ardella replied. She smiled as she pried the lid off the tin. I couldn't see the contents from my position across the table from her.

"Such special memories," Ardella said. "How fortunate I am."

She reached her hand into the tin and her eyes sparkled. She picked something up, but then put it back down, as if having second thoughts. "You know, perhaps I'll tell you the story behind this gift first, then show it to you. To understand the gift, you need to hear the story behind it...What a Christmas that was."

"Sounds good."

Ardella set the tin down and took a long sip of her tea. Then, a thoughtful look crossed her face as she drifted back through the years…

Chapter 6

1908

Sharecropping in the South was a meager living even during the best of years. And 1908 was far from a good year for farming in eastern Virginia's Tidewater Region. The spring rains didn't let up during planting season, then drought took its toll over the long summer months, wiping out fields of crops throughout Lancaster County.

Things were not easy for the Baumgardner family that autumn. Most of the merchants in town would not extend credit to sharecroppers who had no means of paying off debt. Those that did typically wanted collateral—something the Baumgardners lacked.

The Baumgardner family—Ardella, her parents, and younger brother, George—had high hopes when they moved to the Clayton place the previous year. The family that had tilled the land before them had done well enough before heading north for factory work. Old man Clayton had told them so. And he was a man of his word. Mr. Clayton had been kind to the Baumgardners since they moved to his farm.

As hard as the times were, though, the family had a roof overhead and an ample supply of canned vegetables. Ellen

Baumgardner canned tomatoes, peas, cucumbers, and three varieties of beans, all of which were stored in the root cellar. And they had a winter garden: turnips, potatoes and winter squash.

There were eggs from the hen house and there was sweet water from the well. There was seafood too. The tidal creek just down the hill from the house held an ample supply of blue crabs that were easy enough to net. And Ardella's father kept a few crab pots offshore, an easy row in the old skiff that came with the place. The Baumgardners' meals were sometimes supplemented with groundfish that had worked their way into the confines of the crab pots.

George and Ardella contributed to the family larder. They kept two trot lines at the end of the rickety old dock that jutted into the Rappahannock River, just down the hill from the farmhouse. It always amazed them how the blue crabs would cling to the bait, not releasing their grip when the line was hauled in.

The farm was a place of wonders for Ardella and George. In their free time they roamed the fields, hedgerows, marsh and woodlands, looking for arrow heads and musket balls. George once found a Union Army belt buckle. The Union Army had camped on the farm property during the Civil War. An old woman down the road had told them this. She also told them of a small cave in the nearby woods where her family hid when the Yankee gunboats came down the Rappahannock, shelling homes along the shoreline.

Nights at the farmhouse were fun too. Ardella read under the flickering glow of the kerosene lantern. Her mom liked to read as well; her father's favorite pastime was carving. Her father, Horace Baumgardner, spent most evenings quietly working his knife against a slab of softwood, creating birds and other wildlife.

George's passion was marbles. Most nights found him sprawled out in front of the woodstove, a dozen marbles before him encircled by a piece of string. The boy spent countless hours flicking marbles into the circle and edging them outside the string one at a time. Even during those cozy nights inside the farmhouse though, the family's financial situation was never far from their mind.

Mr. Clayton was a humble man who enjoyed sipping sweet tea on the rocking chair on his back porch. He often offered the kids a treat when they were near. The man had a maid, Queeney—a kind, gap-toothed woman who did his cooking and cleaning. Sometimes, Ardella and George helped Mr. Clayton and Queeney. George hauled firewood; Ardella swept the porch floor and front walk.

Toward the end of the summer, old man Clayton was seen on the porch less often. His health began to fail him. Ardella's mother, Ellen Baumgardner, checked in on him often and brought him soup and hot tea. He'd look up at her with a wan smile, his sea-blue eyes thankful.

Come fall the man was barely eating, said he didn't have the appetite. His weight loss was noticeable. The doctor visited him regularly. Mr. Clayton's condition continued to decline. The old man passed on just after Thanksgiving.

The rumor around town was that Mr. Clayton's son up in Winchester had inherited the farm. The Baumgardners had never met him, but they were all too aware of the speculation in town that he'd up and sell the place. With the old man gone now, the family's uncertain future was not lost on any of them. It weighed heavily on the Baumgardners' minds. But they soon had more important worries.

It started during the second week of December. The night George announced he wasn't hungry at dinner. Ordinarily, the boy's hunger was endless.

When Ardella woke the next morning, she glanced across the room to George's bed. He was still fast asleep, very unlike the boy who was always the first to rise. When George didn't come down to the breakfast that morning, Mrs. Baumgardner went to check on him. Ardella watched the concern on her mother's face as she placed the back of her hand against George's brow.

"Oh Lord, he's burning up!"

George's eyes slowly opened. He tried to speak but his voice was raspy. He pointed to his throat and said, "Hurts."

"Don't talk sweetheart. Just rest. Ardella, keep an eye on your brother while I dampen some towels."

The concern on her mother's face was not lost on Ardella. She knew what the sickness could be. She tried to resist the thought, but it was impossible.

Ardella's father hitched the horse to the wagon and headed to town for the doctor. Dr. Lance paid them a visit later that afternoon. By then there was a crimson rash on George's neck. The doctor confirmed their fears. "Scarlet fever."

Ellen Baumgardner gasped; tears welled in her eyes as she raised her hands to her face.

"Just keep doing what you're doing," the doctor instructed. "Apply damp towels to his forehead. Keep him covered, and be sure to give him water. Plenty of water. There's nothing more I can do for him for now. I'll be in Richmond tomorrow, but will stop by when I'm back in town."

Ardella's mother nodded somberly. Her father followed the doctor out. After the doctor had departed, the man tried to busy himself with chores to occupy his mind, though it did little good.

Ardella and her mother continued their vigil by George's bed day and night. George's condition didn't improve. If anything, his health seemed to be declining. Mrs. Baumgardner woke George off and on to give him water. Each time it seemed George struggled more than the time before, just to raise his head and open his mouth.

His mother didn't leave his side. She slept on the floor beside him lest the boy wake in the night. Ardella was there the whole time too, keeping a watchful eye on George and always replacing the towels with fresh ones. She prayed for her little brother.

The doctor returned as promised. Ardella watched his face as he studied George. Ardella was always watching people's faces. There was much to learn from facial expressions. And she didn't like the doctor's expression, though he'd done his best to mask his concern.

The doctor placed a hand on Mrs. Baumgardner's shoulder and said, "You should get some rest. I'll stay with him a while."

She gave a weak smile. "Thank you. But I'm not going anywhere. I want to be right here when he wakes."

Ardella's father, Horace, was in the room now too. "Doc, is there *anything* we can do?" he pleaded.

The doctor shook his head no. "I'm afraid not. Back when I was his age, the doctors used to bleed people in hope of ridding them of the fever, bled them till their lips went pale. That's no longer done though. Only makes a weak body weaker. No, I'm afraid you're doing all you can."

Horace Baumgardner was shaking now. "W-what…What are the chances doctor?"

The doctor placed a hand on Horace's shoulder. "It's not an answer I give. I honestly don't know. The boy is young and strong. This is a plus. Just keep up what you're doing."

Ardella wept uncontrollably. She'd heard every word.

There was still no improvement in George's condition the following day. The fever was deep within the boy. George shook continuously as his mother and sister helplessly maintained their vigil. His father poked his head in the room off and on.

Night descended. George's fever intensified. He let out a few raspy, feverish moans in his sleep.

Ardella woke suddenly, just after sunup. She didn't know

where the sound had come from. Perhaps it had occurred in a dream. Her mom was asleep on the floor beside George. Ardella's eyes moved to George to be sure he was breathing. It had become habit. George's eyes were open. He was looking at her.

"What's the date?" he asked, his voice raspy.

Tears welled in Ardella's eyes. She was too choked up to speak.

"Did you hear me?"

"What?" Ardella smiled, wiping the tears away.

"What's the date?"

"Tuesday."

"No, not the *day*, the *date*."

Ardella glanced at the calendar on the wall. "It's the 15th."

George smiled. "Ten days till Christmas."

George's strength and color returned quickly in the days that followed. The doctor stopped by and confirmed that George had indeed overcome scarlet fever. The boy was soon shooting marbles again.

With George's health on the mend, the Baumgardners turned their thoughts to the holidays. The Saturday before Christmas, Ardella's dad hitched up the horse to the wagon, and Ardella and George hopped in back. They shared an old blanket which they draped over their legs.

They drove across the east field and entered the woodland that bordered the field, following an old cart path. A covey of quail exploded from the undergrowth. Overhead, half a dozen crows called out at the intruders in protest.

Holly bushes were scattered about the forest floor, their vibrant red berries contrasting sharply against the green leaves. They cut some holly branches and pine boughs for a wreath and continued into a small pine grove. Their dad let them choose a tree.

Ardella and George looked over a dozen or so trees before agreeing on a six-footer at the edge of the grove. Their dad removed the ax from the wagon and made quick work of felling the tree. On the way back, Ardella and George sang carols. They had just started singing *The Twelve Days of Christmas* when the wagon cleared the woods and entered the field. A single dove took flight just in front of the wagon.

"Look, a dove!" shouted Ardella.

"Just like in the song," George exclaimed. "Only there were two."

Their dad chuckled. "Maybe it has a mate close by."

"Dad," Ardella inquired. "Do you think that could have been a *turtle dove*?"

Her dad scratched his chin. "Well, I hear they're the same color as that one. And it is the holiday season, so why not? Why, I'll bet that was a turtle dove!"

"Why are turtle doves part of the song?" George inquired. "What do they have to do with Christmas?"

"I think it has something to do with what they symbolize: love and peace."

The three of them looked on as the dove flew across the field. They watched its erratic flight until the bird disappeared over the distant treeline. Ardella and George continued with their song as their dad prodded the horse forward with the reins. It seemed the song had taken on new meaning and they sang with gusto. "On the second day of Christmas…"

Between George's illness and the excitement of the approaching holiday, the Baumgardners had temporarily shut thoughts of their uncertain future from their minds. But that changed on Christmas Eve when Horace Baumgardner returned from town, a somber look on his face. Ardella and George were in the kitchen stringing popcorn with their mom.

Ellen Baumgardner furrowed her brow when she saw the look on her husband's face. "Honey? What's wrong?"

Horace Baumgardner hesitated, not wanting to break up the holiday cheer. But there was no avoiding it. "When I was at the dry goods store this afternoon…I overheard a few guys talking. Seems Mr. Clayton's son is coming to town…Coming down from Winchester…tomorrow. Christmas day. Talk is he's coming to settle his father's affairs and ready the farm for sale."

Ellen was taken aback for a moment, but quickly recovered. "Well, we're not going to let this spoil our holiday. So be it. We are going to *enjoy* this Christmas regardless."

Horace looked at his kids, then kissed his wife on the forehead. "Yes, we will," he said…"though I regret to say that I didn't have money for our traditional Christmas ham. We're just about tapped out."

"We can get by without a ham," Ellen said. "Blue crab will do just fine. We have plenty of that. And we have plenty of vegetables. We'll bake a loaf of bread too. We will get by just fine."

Before going to bed that night, Ardella and George hung their stockings on the beam behind the woodstove. Sleep did not come easily for the two of them, their thoughts on Christmas morning and what treasures, if any, their stockings might hold. In the next bedroom, their parents too found sleep difficult. How much longer the family would have a roof over its head, they did not know.

It was George that woke first Christmas morning. He was back to the old George, full of energy. Ardella wasn't far behind him. They reached their stockings at the same time and spilled the contents onto the floor before the woodstove. There were peaches, apples and pears. There were licorice sticks. And sassafras candy. But what captured Ardella's attention most was the carving in the bottom of her stocking. A turtle dove. George's stocking contained one too.

"It's like the one we saw," Ardella beamed.

"Better," said George.

They were still admiring their freshly carved turtle doves

when there was a knock on the door. Ardella and George approached the door together and opened it. Outside stood an impeccably dressed man. Behind him, a handsome gelding was harnessed to a high-end horse carriage with plush leather seats.

He was a large man. Like his father. It wasn't hard to discern that he was Mr. Clayton's son. The man had the same deep blue eyes and dimpled chin, but his demeanor was more formal.

"Merry Christmas," he said to them matter-of-factly.

Ardella wasn't so sure. "Merry Christmas."

"Are your parents home?"

Just then, Horace and Ellen Baumgardner stepped out to greet the man.

Horace extended his hand. "Horace Baumgardner," he said. "And this is my wife, Ellen. I see you've met my kids, Ardella and young George here."

"Good to meet you all," the man said. "I'm Marvin Clayton."

"We were very sorry to hear about your father," Ellen said. "He was a wonderful man."

"Thank you," Marvin Clayton said, clearing his voice. "I don't mean to interrupt your Christmas, but I'm going to be in town just briefly and there's a matter of business I need to discuss with you."

The Baumgardners braced themselves. How long did they have left? A week? Two weeks? Horace debated sending the kids off to play, to shelter them from the forthcoming news, but decided against it; they'd know soon enough. No sense in delaying the inevitable.

"You're probably aware that I have inherited the farm."

Here it comes.

"My practice and home are up in Winchester. It would be impossible for me to keep up the farm."

Please, no.

"... I'm hoping that you folks will consider staying on. My father always talked very highly of you in his letters. Said he never had harder working folks on the place. I know it's been a tough year, given the drought and all."

Horace Baumgardner was at a loss for words. Ellen Baumgardner stood by her husband, speechless as well.

"In looking at my father's ledgers," the man continued, "I think I may be able to give you a slightly higher cut. And Horace, I own a lumber mill up in Winchester. Could use your help up there in the winter months if you're interested."

Horace Baumgardner's eyes were suddenly watery. He extended his hand. "Mr. Clayton, you have a deal."

"Thank you Mr. Clayton!" Ellen said. "Thank you so very much."

"Please, call me Marvin."

"Marvin, would you like to join us for Christmas dinner?" Ellen asked.

Marvin Clayton smiled. "Yes, but on one condition."

"What's that?"

"I need some help unloading some things from the carriage."

When the Baumgardners walked over to the carriage with Marvin Clayton they were stunned at what they saw. Inside the carriage was a plump Virginia ham, tins of fruits and nuts, assorted pastries, a fruit cake, and several pies. It was a Christmas the Baumgardners would remember forever.

Chapter 7

"That was quite a story," I remarked.

Ardella reached her hand into the tin and extracted a small hand-carved bird. The paint had long ago faded, and there were a number of chips and dents in the wood. She handed it to me with the gentle care one might use with fine crystal.

"The turtle dove?"

"The very one."

It would be hard to imagine the carving as a keepsake if I hadn't heard the story. I couldn't help but admire the craftsmanship. Ardella's father was an artisan. I carefully handed the carving back to her. Ardella glanced fondly at the turtle dove before gently placing it back in the Christmas Tin.

"Glad you enjoyed the story," she said. "That was quite a Christmas. One of my most memorable."

"How old were you?"

Ardella smiled. "A bit younger than you."

"How long did you live on the farm?"

"Almost ten years. Right up until I got married."

"Marvin Clayton never sold the place?"

"No. He ended up moving into his father's old house years later. It became his retirement home."

The dining room staff began bringing plates and utensils out from the kitchen, and the early lunch crowd began to amble into the cafeteria.

"Care to join a lady for lunch?"

I looked up at the clock on the far wall. It was noon. "Sorry," I said. "I need to buy some skates. The ice is waiting for me. But I'd be interested in hearing about the other gifts in the tin some time."

Ardella smiled. "Perhaps next Saturday."

"Look forward to it."

"Go on," she motioned with her hands. "Get yourself some skates and have fun this afternoon!"

"Thanks Ardella."

The warmth of the nursing home—it must have been seventy-five degrees inside—stayed with me for all of three seconds when I stepped outside. The cold cut through my layers of clothes. It took just five minutes to reach the house. I tossed the canvas paper bag in my room, slapped together a peanut butter & jelly sandwich, and ate it on the fly.

The thrift shop was on the opposite side of town. I could already picture the skates tied together and draped over the handlebars of the Schwinn. A nice pair of used Bauers or perhaps Hydes. Maybe even CCM Tacks. Size 8. Back home, I'd sharpen the blades on Dad's grindstone before heading to the pond. I had a whole afternoon of pond hockey ahead of me. Life was good.

I reached the thrift shop in a half hour. The hanging bells on the back of the door announced my arrival as I stepped into the one-room building. An elderly man behind the cash register at the front of the store looked up from his paper and nodded.

"Good afternoon."

"Good afternoon sir," I said, making my way down the narrow center aisle between racks of coats and apparel. I knew right where the skates were: in a large wooden box at the rear of the store.

The box was nearly full. A good sign. Inside the box was a jumble of hockey skates and women's figure skates. I started my search with great anticipation, removing skates, pair by pair, placing them on the floor as I went along in search of size 8 or 9 hockey skates (size 8 would be a perfect fit, but size 9 would work too, if need be, with a little newspaper stuffed in the toe).

Some skates were a few decades old, while others were more modern. There was a practically new pair of Bauer Junior Supremes—only they were two sizes too small. And there was a well worn but very usable pair of Hyde Red Lines. But they were three sizes too big. I still had high hopes when I had gone through half of the skates, though I was all too aware that my chances of finding a pair that fit diminished with each pair I removed. There had to be pair that fit.

I remained hopeful right up until the end, when the bottom of the box became visible. I hadn't counted on this. Pond hockey season was here. The ice was pristine. And I was without skates. I wiped the tears on the sleeve of my jacket as I left the store.

Chapter 8

When I pulled up to the house, I checked the mailbox. There was an envelope from Dad! Nothing in the world beat hearing from Dad, nothing lifted my spirits more. A letter from Dad gave us assurance he was safe—at least at the time he wrote it.

We saw Vietnam on the news every day, and there was always press coverage in the papers, but it was Dad's letters that opened our eyes to life "on the ground" from an infantryman's perspective. He used terms like *hooch*, *water buffalo* and *C-Rations*, and phrases like *in country*. It was through his letters that Mom and I learned bits and pieces about Dad's life over there.

Ripping open the envelope on my way inside the house, I saw there were two letters: one for Mom; one for me. I put Mom's letter on the kitchen table and opened mine.

December 3, 1968
Hey Jess,

How are you doing son? I'm guessing it's about 70 degrees colder where you are right now. I just got back from a patrol a few minutes ago and wanted to write you in time to make the mail run (via helicopter). I hope this letter finds you well.

Mom wrote me about your paper route and how you've been the man of the house. I can't tell you what comfort it brings me. How proud of you I am Jess!

Another day almost over, which means I'm almost one day closer to coming home, "back to the world," as the guys over here say. Can't tell you how I look forward to my final copter ride out of here and hopping on the freedom bird for home. I sure won't miss the food—or the cold showers. But enough complaining. All in all, I've got a lot to be thankful over here. I'm in good company; there are some great guys in our unit. They'd do anything for you.

One of the guys, Tom Blakstone, is from Mashpee, down on Cape Cod. He's has a son about your age. They have a boat and he invited us to do some striper fishing with them when we get back. What do you say to that? Well, I'm going to try to catch a little shuteye now. Over here we take it when we can. Keep up the good work son.

Love Dad
P.S. Did you get a Christmas tree yet?

Nothing turned my mood around like a letter from Dad. I pulled on my boots and jacket, grabbed my hockey stick and gloves from the hallway closet and headed down to the pond.

The guys gave me strange looks when I showed up without skates. They were playing two vs. one. A pair of boots served as goals on each end of the ice. It was Larry against Rob and Jim.

"No luck, huh?" Larry asked, as I approached.

I tapped my stick against the ice, signaling for the puck.

"Nope."

"You can play goalie."

"No," I said. "Pass the puck." I had the utmost respect for goalies but the position wasn't for me. For the remainder of the afternoon, I ran, slipped, and slid up and down the ice, passing the puck, playing offense and defense, trying to keep up with Larry.

To an onlooker it must have been quite a spectacle. But it didn't matter. Dad was safe. And I rode that high for the rest of the day.

Chapter 9

Mom was sitting at the kitchen table, clad in her bathrobe, when I padded into the kitchen on Sunday morning. She seemed lost in thought. Before her lay a flyer from Fiske's Department Store. On the front cover was a picture of a vibrant red Christmas dress. Her eyes were aglow as she sat there transfixed, no doubt thinking of my father.

My parents were very much in love. They had been married on Christmas Eve; their anniversary added an additional element of excitement to the holidays each year. My earliest memories are of them slow dancing before the Christmas tree, looking into each other's eyes. They had always been much more in love than any of my friend's parents, I thought.

"Morning Mom."

"...Oh, good morning honey."

"No coffee?" Mom always had a cup of coffee in front of her when she was in the kitchen.

"No, we're going out for breakfast! What do you say, partner. Up for some breakfast at the diner?"

"You bet! I'll start the truck."

Mom fished through her purse and extracted the Ford key chain. She handed it to me with a smile. "Here you go."

"Thanks, be right back."

During my father's absence, I inherited a number of jobs—small, unnoticed things that he used to do. Chief among them was warming the truck up on cold days. The old Ford F100 three-speed turned over on the third try. Five minutes later, with the heater blasting, the cab was warmer than the house. And we were off to Nick's Diner.

The lot was nearly full when we pulled up in front of the diner. The fogged window glass bespoke the warmth inside Nick's. The diner exuded camaraderie. It was a place where first-time customers felt right at home with the regulars.

With its gumwood veneer, fluted stool columns, hexagonal-tile floor, and original display cases, it was like stepping back in time. Most of the customers that patronized the establishment came for the camaraderie as much as the food.

Upon entering we were greeted by a wave of cacophony: cash register bells, gossip, the clank of plates and silverware. Elvis crooned *Blue Christmas* from a table-top jukebox. Behind the counter, Nick wore a Santa hat, adding to the ambiance.

As was our custom, my mother and I made our way to one of the booths along the far wall, where we could look out at the Berkshire Mountains.

"Hello folks," shouted Maggie, over the din. Maggie was a harbinger of good service. No matter how many customers she had, she always found her way to our table promptly.

"The usual?" she asked, glancing at me as she poured coffee into my mother's mug.

"Yes, thanks Maggie." I said.

"…I think I'll try the banana pancakes today," my mother said, glancing across the room at the specials on the board above the coffee urn.

"Fine choices. Be back shortly folks."

Maggie returned a few moments later and placed a steaming mug of hot chocolate in front of me. "Extra whipped cream, just the way you like it."

"Thanks Maggie."

"Any word from Jack?" she asked my mother.

"Yes, we just received a letter yesterday. He said some of the guys are getting homesick with Christmas approaching."

"God bless all the boys over there. I pray for `em all everyday." Maggie had a brother serving over there.

"As do we, Maggie."

Our occasional Sunday breakfast at the diner was the one thing we splurged on. It was a time for Mom and me to catch up with each other. It was also a time for my mother to address any *issues* that may have arisen during the week.

"I received a call from Principal Wilkins on Friday," she said in her subtle way. "It appears that your teachers are concerned about your grades." I knew immediately that the news pained her.

Mom had always been active in my schooling. In past years she had been on the PTO, served as a parent volunteer and had always been tuned in to my studies and school activities. So much had changed this year. I knew she blamed herself and felt guilty for my poor academic performance.

"I'm sorry Mom." I hadn't considered the effect my indifference toward school work would have on her. A wave of guilt washed over me; my mother had enough troubles without having to worry about me too.

"I know things are different now with your father overseas," she began. "But you need to keep up with your school work. Your dad wouldn't want this."

"I'll do better Mom."

"I know you will, champ. And I know it hasn't been easy on you....I think of him all the time too. Tell you what. From now on, if you ever need any help, we'll review your homework in the morning. Over breakfast."

"You work late Mom. That's not fair to you. "

"No Jesse, it's not fair to *you,* honey. I'm to blame as well. We're in this together."

"Okay."

Just then, Maggie arrived with our food.

We left the warmth and ambiance of the diner forty minutes later and walked into a gusting December wind that penetrated our layers. My mother intertwined her left arm in my right. "How about some window shopping?" she asked. Mom loved to shop, even if it was just looking and not buying.

"You bet," I replied. We trudged uptown, our heads bent

down against the biting wind. Snow swirled over the sidewalk before us.

A sheet of warmth greeted us as we entered Fiske's Department Store. The hanging bells on the entry door announced our arrival. Mom ambled off to the women's department, and I headed upstairs to sporting goods…

They were on the third shelf: a pair of CCM Tacks, size 8. The price tag read $39.99. Hockey season would be long over by the time I was able to save that kind of money. I don't recall how long I stood there admiring the skates, but it was a while. When I turned around, I nearly bumped into Mr. Beauvier. Lost in thought, I had no idea he had been hovering behind me.

"Jesse," he said, matter-of-factly.

"Hi Mr. Beauvier." Never one for small talk, the man headed down the aisle. And then he was gone.

I found Mom a while later in the women's department. She stood transfixed before a red Christmas dress on display—the one advertised in the flyer. Like the skates, it was unaffordable. The price tag read $36.99.

"Hi Mom."

"…Hey kiddo... Ready to hit the road?"

"Yes."

Chapter 10

Sergeant Jack Maclean walked listlessly down the narrow jungle trail. He and the other members of his squad moved ghost-like in the early morning mist as they headed back to the firebase after a night on patrol. They had just cleared the elephant grass and were on the home stretch now, relieved to be back on familiar ground. The perimeter of the hilltop firebase loomed into view through the breaks in the jungle canopy. Five minutes later, the point man gave the password to the GI on guard duty behind the perimeter wire.

The men were on edge after staying alert all night, their nerves like trip wires. Intelligence reports indicated enemy activity in the area, but the night had passed without incident. Once inside the perimeter wire they passed by sandbag bunkers, a howitzer pit, the helicopter landing zone, the CP, and scores of tents the men called "hooches," as they made their way to the mess tent.

Outside the mess tent, the men placed their M16s in the gun rack, then ducked under the flap. Breakfast—dehydrated eggs, bacon, canned milk with oatmeal, and overly strong coffee—was nothing to write home about, but famished men didn't complain. It beat the C-Rations they ate in the field.

Each man grabbed a tray and lined up before the cook at the bench table. The cook doled out generous portions to each man. Men from all over the firebase starting filing into the mess tent; soon a line formed.

Jack took a seat at one of the dozen tables inside the tent and placed his meal before him. Before he lifted his fork though, he pulled out his wallet and extracted a picture of his wife and boy. He placed it in beside his plate where he could look at it as he ate. Hardly a day had passed since he'd been there that he hadn't looked at the picture.

He'd been in country for six months but it seemed an eternity. The world back in Beldon, Massachusetts seemed like a lifetime ago. Like the others he served with, he knew exactly how many days he had remaining until his tour was over.

"Miss `em eh?" The words came from Lonnie Beckwith. Lonnie was a Corporal. He and Jack had met back in Da Nang on their first day in Vietnam. The two had become close friends. Lonnie was a family man too, with a wife and three girls.

"Like crazy."

"I'll drink to that," said Lonnie, raising his coffee cup in a toast.

"Here here," said Jack, lifting his cup.

"Any activity last night?" Lonnie inquired.

"Zilch. It was eerily quiet out there...Too quiet."

"Well, at least you can kick back tonight. My guys and I are heading out at sundown. Going to set up an LP (listening post) four klicks out.

"Keep safe out there."

"I plan to."

They had no way of knowing that an entire enemy regiment was moving down from the north.

Chapter 11

A strange thing happened Tuesday morning before school. The guys and I entered Eugenia's Bakery just as Mr. Beauvier was leaving, coffee in hand. We passed each other at the entrance.

"Morning, Mr. Beauvier," I said.

"Mmmhmm."

As we were waiting for our day-old muffins, which Eugenia kindly provided to us at no charge, Larry said: "That guy used to play semi-pro hockey in Canada back in his prime. On the Canadien's farm team."

"Huh?"

"It's true," Larry confirmed. "My uncle works with him at the mill. He overheard some guy asking him about it in the lunch-room last week."

I was astonished. "I can't believe it." Then I thought back to how the man had predicted the outcome of the Bruins game the other night. I thought about Mr. Beauvier a lot that day. Suddenly I had a lot of questions for the man. I was actually looking forward to his company at dinner that night.

*****

"So…you were a hockey player?" I asked Mr. Beauvier at the supper table. The man chewed thoughtfully and took a sip of milk.

"Mmmhmm."

"No kidding?!"

"Could you pass the potatoes?"

Suddenly there were a hundred questions running through my mind. But then the phone rang. I picked it up. It was Mom. She was on break and just wanted to check in. We just talked for a few minutes. When I hung up, Mr. Beauvier was scraping his plate over the sink. Then he retired to his room. My questions would have to wait.

After dinner, I immersed myself in homework. I found it actually helped remove my thoughts from my father's situation. I buckled down at school that week. And my efforts seemed to be paying off, from the approving nod Principal Wilkins gave me in the hallway a few days later. He *knew*.

On Thursday, after my paper route, I played hockey on foot with the guys down at the pond. I got home a little later than usual. Mr. Beauvier had already finished dinner. I took my dinner to the living room. The Bruins were playing the Rangers that night and Mr. Beauvier was seated in Dad's recliner. Interestingly, it didn't bother me. The opening face off was five minutes away.

"So, you played hockey up in Canada?"

"…Mmmhmm."

"When?"

"…Back in the 30's."

"You played semi-pro? On the Canadien's farm team?"

"That's right."

"Did you ever play pro?"

Mr. Beauvier winced. "... Yes."

"You did!?"

"One game."

"Could you tell me about it?" This was truly astonishing.

"Not much to tell...Well, the Canadiens coach, Cecil Hart, was talking with our farm team coach during practice one day. This was the fall of 1936. November. After practice, my coach called me over and introduced me to Cecil. Cecil said he wanted me to attend a few practice sessions with the Canadiens. The pro team. Well, I did. And after three practices, Cecil informed me that I was to suit up for the upcoming game against Chicago."

"I had never been in better shape or more prepared for a game, though my nerves were taught and there was queasiness in my stomach. I didn't sleep but a few hours the night before, with all the anxiety. One of the guys next to me on the bench, Babe Siebert, took a look at me and said: 'Don't worry rook. You're first game jitters will pass soon as you're on the ice.'"

"Cecil put me in toward the end of the first period. Babe was right. My jitters were gone as soon as I was in motion. I played for five glorious minutes...Until the injury."

"What happened?"

"...I was a defenseman. I was going behind our net to clear the puck. I had just cleared the puck up ice when I was cross-checked into the boards by their winger, a real beefy guy. It was a real hard hit; the guy really had some momentum going. I later heard the guy was taking revenge from getting body-checked by one of our guys earlier in the game. My leg somehow twisted when I made contact with the boards…I heard a snap. Next thing I know I'm down on the ice."

"Wow. Did you play again when your leg healed?"

"…No. My leg didn't heal quite right. I tried, but I'd lost my speed. It was never the same. My window of opportunity was gone."

I didn't know what to say. It was the longest conversation I ever had with the man, would ever have. Mr. Beauvier never again talked about his hockey career. We watched the Bruins take on the Rangers on Channel 38 that night in comfortable silence.

Chapter 12

Saturday was the coldest day yet. It was sixteen degrees out when I started the route that morning. The warmth of the nursing home was a welcome reprieve from the weather when I finally arrived. One of morning-shift nurses informed me that Ardella was in the cafeteria. After delivering the papers to my other customers, I left Ardella's paper by her front door and found her in the cafeteria at the same table as before. She was wearing dark slacks and a white sweater with a Christmas tree embroidered on the front. The Christmas Tin was on the table, resting beside a pot of tea and two cups.

"My, how cold you look Jesse," she said when I stepped into the room. "Come, sit. We'll get some hot tea in you."

"That sounds real good."

The tea was *wonderful*. After battling the cold all morning, it was just what I needed. It was good to see Ardella; she had quickly become my favorite customer. We caught up a bit. I told her about the recent letter from Dad, of breakfast at the diner with Mom, and a little about my week at school.

"So, do have time for another story?" I inquired.

She smiled. "Time is something I seem to have a lot of these days."

Ardella took a sip of tea. Then she removed the lid from the Christmas Tin and peered inside it for a few moments. "There was another Christmas on the farm that comes to mind. Would you like to hear it?"

"Yes, I would."

Ardella placed the lid on the table beside the tin, closed her eyes, and drifted back over the years once again…

Chapter 13

November 30, 1910

The old woman's pace was slow and methodical. It had not varied since she began her journey—just after daybreak. She was clad in a faded cotton dress and a wide-brimmed straw hat. Strapped over her right shoulder was a weathered canvas bag. Like her dress, the bag held many patches.

It was mid-afternoon when the elderly African-American woman turned off the county road and stepped onto the farm lane. Ardella and George were stacking firewood on the front porch of the cottage when they saw the old woman slowly advance down the lane. She was a curious sight. Visitors were rare on the farm; those that did stop by typically arrived via horse-drawn wagon or buggy rather than making the long trek down the lane on foot.

There were only two residences on the farm—the Baumgardners' cottage and Marvin Clayton's white-columned Federal-style home located at the end of the lane. As the woman slowly passed by, George and Ardella assumed she was going to visit Mr. Clayton. He wasn't home though. The man was tending to business up in Winchester.

They were about to run over to let her know that Mr. Clayton was out of town, but the woman surprised them. She stepped off the farm lane and walked onto the field that bordered it. Then she walked across the field toward the dense growth at the far edge that separated the field from the woodland beyond.

Ardella and George looked on as the woman cut across the field, her methodical pace even slower now on softer ground. When the woman finally reached the far side, she didn't stop. She walked into the dense growth past the field… and disappeared into it. Now Ardella and George were really curious.

There was nothing in the growth, they knew, except for a row of six old dilapidated cabins in a small clearing. Ardella and George had explored the area when they first moved to the farm. The cabins were from another time. All of them had stick-and-mud chimneys and were in various stages of decay. The roofs were caved in on several of the structures; all of them were choked in briers and weeds.

The cabins had always been mysterious to Ardella and George. Most were bereft of furnishings, though a few contained old sleeping pallets, wooden barrels, cast iron cooking pots, stump stools and other rough handcrafted furniture. Weeds and vines poked up between floor boards, and sunlight penetrated through holes in the roofs. The cabins obviously hadn't been occupied in decades.

Ardella and George headed across the field. When they reached the far edge and peered into the growth, there was no sign of the old woman. They followed a deer trail into the cover. The trail meandered a bit and eventually brought them to the small clearing with the cabins. The old woman was on her hands and knees beside the last cabin. She was clearing brush away from something. A stone…A grave.

They watched in silence for a few minutes as the woman continued to labor. "I know you're there," she called out. "I may be old, but I've still got my hearing."

Ardella and George froze. The woman looked up at them and smiled. "Hello there young'uns."

"Hi ma'am," said Ardella. "I'm Ardella and this is my brother George. We live in the cottage."

"Indeed you do. I saw you on my way here."

"What are you doing?" George inquired.

"Tidyin' up. And payin' my respects. Two things I've had a mind to do for a long time."

"I can help you clear that brush," George offered.

"That would be fine. Just fine."

"And I'll get you some water," Ardella offered.

The woman wiped her brow and flashed another smile. "I wouldn't say no to that."

George and the old woman had cleared a three-foot perimeter around the grave when Ardella returned carrying a jar of cool spring water. Ardella handed the woman the jar. She sat down and savored the cool water.

"Much obliged."

George and Ardella looked at the grave. It was just a plain stone bereft of any markings.

"There's no lettering or dates," George remarked.

The woman took another long pull from the jar. Then she said, "Nobody owned a stone chisel. The lettering was done in charcoal."

"Charcoal?" Ardella inquired.

"Yes. We made do with a piece of charcoal from the fireplace. Was all we had."

"But everything must've washed off in the first rainstorm after that," George said.

"Indeed it did. But it doesn't matter. It's up here," the woman said, pointing to her head. "I remember everything. Including the date."

The woman shifted her position and faced the stone. It was obviously of great significance to her, this gravestone. She reached into her canvas shoulder bag and extracted a red poinsettia flower. Then she gently placed it at the base of the grave.

Ardella glanced around for some wildflowers. Nothing was in bloom at this time of year, but she did locate a few stray sunflowers and purple asters that still had some color to them. She picked the flowers and placed them next to the poinsettia. The old woman's face creased in yet another smile. "Old Nathaniel would like that," she remarked.

Over the next hour, the woman pointed things out, things from a previous time. The slope behind the cabins where trash was discarded. An old fire pit. Garden plots long since surrendered to thicket. And she mentioned the names of children that had lived in the cabins.

"Where did the kids go to school?" George inquired.

The woman looked at him, her face unreadable. "Slave children didn't attend school."

The wind had picked up gradually since they arrived. It rustled the trees behind the cabins. Then the sky darkened and it started to drizzle. "Come home with us," Ardella implored. "To our cottage. You can have dinner with us."

The old woman hesitated. "That's a right kind offer, but I'll be fine. Best be moving on. If the two of you could accompany me back to the lane though, I'd be grateful. It was hard going a-cross the stubble."

"We'd be glad to," Ardella said. The woman took a long, final look around. Then the three of them left the clearing and navigated their way back to the field, George on one side of the woman, Ardella on the other.

Ardella's mother was working the hand pump at the well in front of the cottage when she saw her children and the old woman coming up the lane. "Hello there," she called out. "I see you've met my kids."

The old woman looked peaked after the trek across the field, but her countenance remained cheerful. "Indeed I have. You have two fine young'uns here. They blessed me with their pre-sence."

Ardella's mother walked over and extended her hand. "I'm Ellen."

The old woman clasped her hand. "Matilda."

"Do you live in town, Matilda?"

"No. I'm visiting with my sister over in Irvington."

"You *walked* here from Irvington?"

"That I did. Started just after sunup."

The drizzle turned to light rain. Ellen Baumgardner looked up at the sky. "I was about to get some vegetables for supper. We'd be honored if you joined us. It's just about ready."

"Mom's making oyster pie," George put in.

The old woman hesitated. Then she too looked up at the sky. "Well, it has been a long day. Yes. I'd be grateful to sit for a spell. Thank you kindly."

Horace Baumgardner had spent the day clearing brush around the perimeter of the farm's east field, in an effort to squeeze in additional rows of corn for the next planting season. He made it back to the house just in time for dinner. The kids introduced their father to Matilda, and he too welcomed her.

Over dinner, it was decided that Matilda would spend the night. She politely declined the offer at first, not wanting to be a bother. But the Baumgardners insisted, and she eventually relented.

"The mechanic in town is headed to Irvington in the morning to pick up supplies," Horace informed her. "I'll bring you to town first thing in the morning, and you can catch a ride with him."

"That would be just fine, if it's not too much bother."

"No bother at all. I'm heading to town anyway."

"Thank you kindly."

After dinner, Ellen made tea for the adults, and everyone settled in the cottage's small living room. Rain softly pelted the tin roof. Horace got a fire going in the wood stove, and George spread his marbles out on the floor in front it.

"How come you left a poinsettia at Nathaniel's grave?" George asked. "Why not a rose or a carnation?" It was so like George to ask a question out of the blue, hours after making an observation.

Matilda smiled. "The poinsettia is a Christmas flower. Old Nathaniel was all about Christmas. I think he would have liked it."

"Who was Nathaniel?" Ellen asked.

"He was the man I came to pay my respects to today."

"His grave is across the field, in the thicket by the old cabins," George explained.

"The old slave quarters?" Horace inquired.

Matilda stared into the embers in the wood stove. "Yes sir."

"He must have been very special for you to come all this way," Ellen remarked.

"Indeed he was."

"Could you tell us about Nathaniel?" Ardella asked.

"Ardella, I'm sure Matilda is tired after her long journey," her father cut in.

Matilda's face creased in a slow grin. "That's okay. I'm

not ready to turn in just yet…It was a long time ago. But yes, I'll tell you about Nathaniel. His is a story that deserves to be told…"

Chapter 14

1850

The driver pulled back on the reins and brought the horse-drawn wagon to a stop before the row of cabins. A harvest moon illuminated the nightscape. Matilda, her younger sister, Lily, and her parents took in the new surroundings as the driver hopped down from the buckboard and lowered the wagon's tailgate. The journey down from the Barre Plantation in Northumberland County was only thirty-something miles as the crow flies, yet it had taken nearly two days to reach this plantation, the Whitestone Plantation.

Matilda's family was to live and work at the Whitestone Plantation through the first of the year, an arrangement made by the owner of the Barre Plantation to fund a gambling debt. It was a common agreement, the hiring out of one's slaves.

The foursome slowly disembarked from the wagon, their joints stiff from the long ride. Each carried a small burlap sack that contained the minimal clothing and few odd personal items they owned. "You folks are in the fifth cabin." The driver gestured with his hand.

Matilda and Lily trailed behind their parents, the earth cool and moist against the soles of their feet. They tentatively followed their parents inside. The dim glow from a grease lamp provided just enough light to reveal the simple contents of the one-room dwelling: two sleeping pallets, an old quilt, two stump stools, a cast iron pot, and a makeshift table—a board placed over two wooden barrels. But even in the dim light, it was evident the place was a vast improvement over their former residence. There were planks on the floor rather than dirt. And the place was dry. There was even glass in the windows.

The next morning, Matilda and Lily headed off to the tobacco field with the adults. But when they arrived, surprisingly, they were informed them that they were too young for field work. Their job would be to bring water to those working in the field. It was a welcome surprise for ten-year-old, Matilda. She had already put in thousands of hours toiling in the fields at the Barre Plantation; she had been sent to the fields on her eighth birthday. Lily too.

They quickly learned that the Whitestone Plantation was indeed a different kind of place. The weekly food allotment was far more nourishing and generous than what they were accustomed to receiving. And the working conditions were a most welcome change from the harsh conditions on the old plantation, where the overseer presided over their every movement, whip at the ready. Here, the adults worked in the fields five days a week rather than the typical six. This was a blessing in itself.

Weekends on this plantation were spent tending to their own garden plots and catching up on household chores. And for the first time in their lives, Matilda's parents had an opportunity to make money. Here, they could gather walnuts in the woodland and sell them at the market in town on weekends, along with handmade brooms and other handcrafted items.

The families that lived in the cabins were a tight-knit community, and they welcomed Matilda's family. The families helped one another. Each household contributed to the small community in some way. There was a midwife. And there was an older woman in one of the middle cabins that healed ailments with herbs from the surrounding fields and woodland. One of the men had a way with gardens, knew how to grow robust crops. He shared his crops with those in the other cabins. Another woman wove cloth and patched clothes. One woman cut hair. And then there was the storyteller.

On Saturday evenings, the families would gather around the fire pit, and the storyteller would regale everyone with a tale. Some of the men played musical instruments during this time. Matilda's father played a jaw harp.

One Sunday, Matilda and Lily were playing with the kids who lived in the adjacent cabins, when a tall man ambled down the path and stepped into the clearing. He carried a burlap sack over his shoulder. The man smiled when he saw the barefoot children; he made his way over to them.

"Hello young'uns," the man exclaimed. He knelt down and lowered the sack to the ground. "I see some new faces," he said, directing his attention to Matilda and Lily. "Welcome." He then reached into the bag and extracted a handful of walnuts. He handed three walnuts to each child. After that, he stood up and made his way to the last cabin in the row and slipped inside.

"That was Nathaniel," one of the children informed Matilda. "He works for the blacksmith in town. He sleeps in the blacksmith shop during the week. Spends Sundays here with his wife."

Sometimes, in the weeks that followed, Nathaniel brought the children rock candy; once he even brought peaches. Nathaniel was a friend to the children; he regaled them with old African folk tales that his grandfather had told him as a boy. And he told them stories of his boyhood on a plantation further south. To his credit, he had a way of diplomatically settling the occasional disputes that cropped up among the children, always with a smile.

Matilda, Lily and the other children eagerly looked forward to Nathaniel's Sunday visits. They were the highlight of their week. Nathaniel's visits continued all summer and into the fall, even though it was a seven mile walk from the blacksmith shop in town. But on the last Sunday in November, Nathaniel didn't show up. Nor he did arrive on the following Sunday or the one after that.

The children waited for Nathaniel each week, to no avail. Winter was approaching, and they were still barefoot; only the adults had shoes. The adults needed them for working in the fields. But it hadn't snowed yet, and so far the children were able to get by, though their feet were getting colder with each passing day.

In mid-December, the children overheard the reason why Nathaniel no longer returned on the Sabbath each week: he was working Sundays. And the strange part was that it was his doing. The man had volunteered to work Sundays. It was unheard of. Sunday had been his only day off. Nobody understood it.

As the holidays approached, a pall hung over Matilda's family. An uneasiness set in. Their time at the Whitestone Plantation was growing short, they were all too aware. It had been good living in this place, among these people. They knew they would only be there until the first of January. That had been the deal. As the days grew shorter, so too did their hopes. None of them had any desire to return to the plantation back in Northumberland County. Back to those wretched conditions, back to working under the scrutiny of the harsh overseer, with hardly a minute of time for themselves.

On Christmas Eve, the family was seated around the hearth. Matilda and Lily were crafting corn husk ornaments while their parents talked softly. A knock on the door interrupted the quietude. Matilda's father opened the door. It was Nathaniel. He was holding two small packages. "Good evenin'. I have gifts for the young'uns."

"Nathaniel!" Matilda and Lily were so excited to see him again.

"Come in, come in," said Matilda's father.

“Hello missies.” Nathaniel kneeled down and handed each of them a package. The wrapping was nothing fancy, just brown paper bound with string. Matilda and Lily opened their presents at the same time. “Shoes!”

They had never before owned a pair of shoes. The two of them were awestruck, as were their parents. Matilda and Lily hugged the man, while their parents thanked Nathaniel profusely.

“Well,” Nathaniel said, “I should be movin’ on. I have more deliveries to make.” They would later learn that Nathaniel had sacrificed his Sundays to make shoes for the children, had struck a deal that allowed him to use the cobbler’s tools and leather remnants after hours, in exchange for his labor on Sundays.

A few minutes after Nathaniel departed, Matilda and Lily were proudly walking around the cabin, staring down at their new shoes, when there was another knock on the door. Their father opened the door to see the plantation owner, Mr. Whitestone, and his young son standing outside. Each of them held a bundle of clothing: trousers, winter jackets, hats, linen shirts and socks.

“Seasons Greetings,” said Mr. Whitestone.

“And to you,” replied Matilda’s father. “Please, come in.”

The Whitestones stepped inside the cabin. The father and his son distributed clothing to all four of them. Matilda’s family stared at the clothing in wonderment. The clothing was completely unexpected, particularly since they would be leaving so soon.

“Thank you,” Matilda’s mother said. “We’ll miss this place.”

Mr. Whitestone's eyebrows arched in a friendly manner. "Miss it?"

"Yes," Matlida's father cut in. "We were told of the a-greement. We know we're only here until January first."

The man smiled. "On the contrary. I guess you didn't hear the news. I've been in touch with the owner of the plantation up in Northumberland County. We settled on a new agreement. You folks are entitled to stay on, remain here...permanently. That is, if it's okay with you."

Matilda and Lily beamed. Their parents were smiling too.

*****

An ember popped in the fireplace and brought everyone's thoughts back to the present. Ardella was the first to speak. "Were you here during the war?"

Matilda seemed still lost in thought at first. But then she responded. "Yes. The Confederates camped here on their way north. And later on the Yankees came. They camped here for a night too when they passed through. This farm you live on now was just a small part of the plantation. The plantation was sold not long after the war. The land was divided up."

"Did you move north after President Lincoln signed the Emancipation Proclamation?" Ardella inquired.

Matilda shook her head no. "We stayed on and worked for wages. Mr. Whitestone and the mistress had always been good to us. We had what we needed here. We were better off than many of those at the other plantations or in slave refugee camps. We stayed on until Mr. Whitestone passed on and the place was sold. By then I was married and had two young'uns, another on the way. My family settled in Richmond after that."

A few moments passed as the Baumgardners digested the story. Then George broke the silence. "What's a corn husk ornament?"

Matilda grinned. "If you can scrounge up some corn husks, I'll show you."

"Be right back!"

George raced out to the corn crib. He returned a few minutes later with a handful of corn husks. He handed them to Matilda.

"Okay," Matida said. "Now we just need a little water and a towel to dampen them with. And perhaps a piece of string and a scrap of ribbon if you have it."

Ardella retrieved a spool of string, a strip of red ribbon and a kitchen towel, while George went to the well for a cup of water. Then they brought everything to the kitchen table and gathered around Matilda. They watched as the woman dampened the husks and shaped them into ball-shaped ornaments, binding each with string, then garnishing them with ribbon.

Matilda made two ornaments. One for George and one for Ardella. "For your Christmas tree," she smiled, handing an ornament to each of them.

"I'll get more corn husks," George said.

"That would be fine."

They never saw Matilda again after their father brought her to town the following morning. But Ardella and George would think of her each holiday season as they crafted corn husk ornaments.

Chapter 15

Once again, I had become totally absorbed in one of Ardella's stories. It had been a welcome distraction. I was already looking forward to her next story.

Ardella reached into the tin and gently extracted a frayed ball-shaped ornament adorned with a faded red ribbon. She carefully placed it in my palm. The corn husk was quite brittle; I was amazed the ornament was still intact.

"Is this the one Matilda made for you?" I inquired.

"It is."

"Remarkable."

After admiring it, I cautiously handed the ornament back to Ardella. She took great care in returning it to the tin. Then the early crowd arrived at the cafeteria.

"Well," Ardella said. "Have fun on the ice this afternoon."

"Thanks." I hadn't told her about my skate dilemma. "See you Monday."

"I look forward to it."

*****

The heavy rain had abated earlier that afternoon, but the sky remained overcast as daylight ebbed. There would be no moon, no stars visible overhead. It would be a dark night for those on guard duty in the sandbag bunkers inside the small hilltop firebase.

Sergeant Jack Maclean was among those on guard duty. He shared a bunker with a private from Kansas City, a new kid that had just arrived that week.

Nights like this one, Jack knew, were favorable for the enemy. The wet ground muted their footfalls. The enemy could inch his way to the perimeter undetected, cut the wire, and slip in under the cover of darkness.

But the Americans had taken precautions. That afternoon they'd set up flares on trip wires in the open terrain between the perimeter of the base and the jungle. Those in the sandbag bunkers were alert.

It was 2:00AM when the first flare went off, illuminating the nightscape… exposing the forward platoon of an entire enemy regiment. Seconds later a second flare went off, revealing more enemy troops moving in from the east. Then a third flare ignite-ed…A dozen NVA soldiers slipped under the wire. There were many more behind them.

The private leaped out of the bunker and ran toward the rear of the base. Jack remained in place, his M16 resting on the edge of the bunker, pointed at the first wave of enemy troops…

Chapter 16

"Let's go get a tree," Mom announced. It was Sunday morning. She had made pancakes for breakfast, and I was just finishing my last one. Nobody made pancakes like Mom.

"I'll start the truck," I announced.

Five minutes later we were en route to Jenkins Farm. Jenkins Farm was situated on the eastern edge of town; a ten-minute ride from our place.

We had cut our Christmas tree at Jenkins Farm each December for as long as I could remember. One of my earliest memories was of Dad carrying me on his shoulders, ax in hand, as we cut across the fields to the farm's woodlot. It sure felt different without Dad there.

After stopping by the farm stand to say hello to the Jenkins and drink a cup of hot cider, Mom and I headed down the farm lane that divided the orchards from the fields. The scene before us could have been a Currier & Ives print: a red barn beside a stone farmhouse and a skating pond, backdropped by the Berkshire Mountains.

Several families were skating on the pond as we passed by. In years past, that would have been Mom, Dad and I. The

Jenkins always placed a few benches around the pond, and there was a small lean-to where one could warm up on blustery days. Mom always brought a thermos of hot chocolate for our skating excursions.

"We didn't think to bring our skates," Mom said.

"Next time," I said. I hadn't told her that my skates no longer fit. She had enough on her mind.

We were in no great hurry when we reached the woodlot. The temperature was a balmy forty-two degrees, and the sun was breaking through the clouds. We had the place to ourselves and took our time meandering among the rows. Mom and I split up for a while. I caught up with her along the western edge of the lot. She was standing in front of a thick Douglas fir. It was a fine tree with soft, bluish-green needles; I could smell the pine-like fragrance from where I stood.

"How old?" She asked, pointing to the tree.

"Hmmm…Well. An eight footer would be around six or seven years old. I'd say this one is a bit less than eight feet. It's probably around five and a half years old," I stated.

"You're father taught you well. He'd be proud."

I smiled. Dad worked on a tree farm as a teenager. And he knew his Christmas trees. Aside from growth rates, he was full of facts and information about the various types of trees. Hearing Dad's thoughts and theories on the subject of Christmas trees was something we looked forward to each holiday season. He'd always mention that the Jenkins were smart to plant Douglas firs because they grew faster than some other trees and they grew cone-shaped naturally.

"What do you think of it?" Mom asked.

"That's the one."

It started to snow ten minutes later as we dragged the tree back to the truck. The snow intensified as we pulled away from the farm. And I found myself finally starting to get into the Christmas spirit.

*****

When we got home, Mom set up the tree stand in the corner of the living room, while I dragged the tree into the house. After we wrestled the tree into the stand and set it upright, I filled the stand with water. Then we stepped back and admired it.

"One of the best ever," Mom said. "Perhaps *the* best."

"For sure."

"...Your father would be delighted," Mom said, a touch of sadness in her tone.

"I was just thinking of Dad, too." He loved Christmas.

"We'll take a picture and send it to him," Mom said. "After we decorate it. Speaking of decorating, we'll let the branches settle a bit first. We can decorate it next weekend. I've got to be at the hospital for the afternoon shift."

"It's Sunday, Mom. Your day off." Mom never worked Sundays.

"Yes, sorry, sport. I'm covering for a co-worker. I'm off next weekend though. I'll leave dinner on the stove for you and Mr. Beauvier for tonight."

"Thanks Mom. Be careful driving."

"I will honey."

My mind flashbacked to installing snow tires on the truck with Dad back in July, just before he shipped out. "They'll make for a rough ride until it snows, but I'll sleep better over there come winter knowing that the snow tires are on," Dad said.

Even with the traction afforded by the snow tires, I worried about Mom driving back from work. I stayed up well past midnight, until I saw the truck's headlights illuminate the driveway. The snow had not abated.

*****

I woke up an hour earlier than usual Monday morning. The neighborhood was blanketed in white, and the snow was still slanting down. The truck was buried under a foot of snow. I made my way into the kitchen and turned on the transistor radio on the counter beside the sink. "No school, for all schools in the following towns…Adams…Athol…Balfour…Beldon…"

Snow day!

It was only 6:15AM. I went back to bed and caught up on my sleep. Later that morning, after a leisurely breakfast, I helped Mr. Beauvier shovel his car out. Then I shoveled the driveway and cleared the snow off the truck.

I got a much earlier start than usual on the paper route. Even though I delivered the papers on foot, I reached Beldon Manor at two o'clock that afternoon. The parking lot had been plowed, but the front walk hadn't been touched. It was buried under a foot of snow.

As I made my way up the walk, the nursing coordinator opened the front entry door and called out to me. "Good to see you!"

"Thanks." I continued up the walk.

"We're in a bit of a bind," the woman said. "The contractor that plows the parking lot usually brings a helper to shovel the walk. As you can see, this didn't happen today. I wanted to ask if you'd like the job. We'd pay you of course."

"Sure."

"Great. There's a snow shovel in the janitor's closet."

It took twenty minutes to shovel the front walk and the steps. There was a bucket of rock salt beside the nursing home's entrance. After I finished shoveling, I liberally applied rock salt to the walk and steps. Then I shouldered the canvas bag of papers and entered the nursing home.

The nursing coordinator was at the front desk. She was

talking on the phone but raised her hand, gesturing me to stop. She hung up a few minutes later and reached into the one of the front desk's drawers. The woman removed an envelope entitled PETTY CASH. She extracted a ten-dollar bill. "Thanks for your help," she smiled, handing me the money.

"No problem. Thank *you*!"

"The job is yours next storm if you're available."

"I'll be here. You can count on it."

I glanced into the sitting room on the way down the hall. Surprisingly, the television was off. Ardella and a half dozen other patrons were chatting as they hung ornaments on the Christmas tree. One of the nurses had brought an extra box of ornaments from home.

"What a welcome surprise," Ardella said, when she saw me. "Didn't expect you so early."

"Snow day. No school."

"Lucky you."

Ardella introduced me to the others. I actually joined in and hung a few ornaments. As we decorated the tree, Ardella praised me before her friends as if I were a favorite grandson. I'd be remiss if I said I didn't enjoy the attention.

After the box of ornaments had been emptied, I said to Ardella: "I've got some time today if you have time for another story."

Ardella beamed. "Indeed I do. In fact, I could tell it here, in this room. That way, my friends here could listen too, if there's interest." Everyone in the room nodded. During her last story, I had noticed several patrons in the cafeteria glancing at us now and then. They seemed curious.

"Jesse, could you get the Christmas Tin from my room?"

"You bet. Be right back."

One of the nurses set up folding chairs in a half-moon formation. When I returned with the Christmas Tin, everyone was seated. Ardella was sitting in a chair facing the small audience. I handed the tin to her and took a seat with the others.

Unlike the other times, Ardella did not remove the lid from the tin and peer inside. Instead, she placed the Christmas Tin on the floor in front of her, for all to see. "This story will likely be a bit longer than the other two," she stated, directing her attention toward me.

"I'm in no hurry to go back outside."

"Very well then, I'll get underway. This story goes back to the 1930's, during the Depression—"

"Wait," I interrupted. "Would it be possible to see the gift first this time?" I had grown quite curious about the gifts inside the tin by this time.

Ardella smiled. "You're looking at it."

"Huh?"

Ardella gestured to the tin. "Today I'm going to tell the story *of* the Christmas Tin."

"Oh," I said, not exactly understanding.

And then she began…

Chapter 17

December 1933

The old Model T rambled down Route 66 past yet another group of tarpaper shacks. Every state they passed through had these shack colonies. There had been so many of them since leaving Hampton Roads. People called them "Hoovervilles."

Ardella Baumgardner Calder glanced out the window. Eight months pregnant, she and her growing family were eager to get settled in California. The boys, seven year-old Randolph Jr. and four year-old Jimmy, were in back. Her husband, Randolph, was behind the wheel, hunched forward, eyes focused intently on the road.

Up ahead, along the edge of the road, stood a young girl and her mother. The girl was holding a sign: NEED FOOD. The family inside the old Model T wasn't much better off. They needed every penny if they were going to make it out west.

Randolph pulled the Ford over to the side of the road and stopped. Ardella reached into the bushel basket of peaches on the floor. She picked out two peaches, opened the door, and handed them to the mother.

"I'm sorry we can't give more," Ardella told the woman.

The woman smiled. "Bless you. This is a help. Godspeed to you."

"And to you."

Randolph pulled forward, and they continued down the road. As they drove on, Ardella reflected back on the past year. The Depression hadn't affected the Calder family as early as some of the other families back in Hampton Roads. They had survived the first years of the Depression relatively unscathed. Randolph had been a foreman at the H.C. Clovis Machine Shop. He had worked there for twelve years, had always been good with his hands. As a teenager, he had apprenticed as a blacksmith. That H.C. Clovis closed his machine shop at the end of August, after the hurricane, came as no surprise. The shop was barely making a go of it as it was, like so many other businesses. The hurricane damage just speeded up the inevitable.

Randolph had moonlighted as a waterman for years, tonguing oysters and crabbing; he could have done that full time had the skiff not been demolished in the hurricane. Folks in the Chesapeake Bay region referred to the hurricane as *the storm of the century*.

For three months after the closing of the H.C. Clovis Machine Shop, Randolph traveled through four counties, seeking employment. But there was no work to be had. The nation's unemployment rate stood at twenty-five percent.

When Randolph's cousin in California called with an offer of part-time garage work, it was too good to pass up. Part-time work was far better than no work. A lot of families were fleeing to California, most of them hoping to find migrant farm work.

The Calders could pick crops too to get by should the garage job not pan out. Hard work was not new to them.

They were on a barren stretch of Route 66, past Tulsa, when the old Ford suddenly slowed. At first they thought it was just another flat tire. The Model T had suffered six flat tires since leaving Virginia. But then they saw the steam emanating from the hood. Randolph pulled over to the side of the road and disembarked with his toolkit. The boys got out too, eager to help. They watched as their father slid underneath the car.

Randolph got up and walked over to Ardella's side of the vehicle a few minutes later. The boys followed. "Bad news. The radiator is shot."

"Can you patch it?"

Randolph, the man who could do anything with his hands, shook his head. "It needs to be welded. I've got my welding iron but it's useless without solder and a metal plate. Best I can do is plug it to hold enough water to get us a few more miles. We'll let her cool down while I whittle a plug. Then we'll dump the remainder of the water in and try to get a few more miles down the road. Try to find some help."

Dusk was fast approaching, and the temperature started to drop. Randolph pulled out his pocketknife and looked around for something to use as a plug. An old log half buried in a roadside ditch caught his eye.

The boys followed their father and watched as he shaved a piece of wood from the log and whittled it down with his pocket-knife. And they looked on as Randolph hammered the small cone-shaped plug into the radiator. Then it started to rain.

"Back to the car," Randolph told the boys. He poured the last of the water into the radiator, cranked the hand crank at the front of the car, then ran back and hopped into the driver's seat. The old Ford lurched slowly forward

Randolph drove on, one hand on the wheel, the other working the hand-operated windshield wiper. The headlights provided little illumination through the rain, which was coming down in earnest. Ardella prayed they'd come across civilization before the water ran out. A mom & pop motel, a roadside diner, a gas station…anything.

This stretch of Route 66 was relatively flat, but there was a slight rise in the distance, barely discernible in the slanting rain. If the water in the radiator held out, they might reach it and coast downhill for a while. Perhaps there was a town over the rise.

Everyone held their breath as the Model T neared the rise. Two hundred yards…a hundred yards…fifty yards. The old Ford struggled up the rise, steam spewing from the hood.

Their hopes rapidly diminished when they crested the rise and saw no signs of life beyond it. No lights. No businesses or eating establishments. No automobiles. No people. The Model T descended, gaining momentum at first, then slowing as the road leveled out. Still no sign of life…except a lone mailbox along the right side of the road fifty yards ahead. Behind it was an over-grown driveway.

"We're not going to make it much further," Randolph said, his hands tightly gripping the wheel, his knuckles white. "I'll pull over up ahead into that driveway."

Gravel crunched under the tires as the Model T pulled off the road and onto the rough driveway. The driveway wound through scrub brush. About twenty yards in, the car came to a rolling stop, steam bursting from the radiator.

Randolph pulled on his slicker. "Boys, you take care of your Mom. I'm going to see what's up the driveway. See if there might be some shelter."

Ardella squeezed his hand. "Be careful sweetheart."

Randolph gave her a peck on the forehead. "Be back in a jiffy."

Rain pelted the roof as Ardella and the boys watched Randolph disappear up the driveway. The minutes ticked by like hours as they waited. The rain intensified even more. The three of them jumped when lightning flashed. Then came the thunder. A second flash of lightning illuminated the landscape. In that split second, Ardella saw a house and a barn up the driveway, about seventy yards away. Randolph was in front of the house talking to someone. An old woman it appeared. Then the night was black again. The image was gone.

Randolph jogged down the overgrown driveway back to car. Rain slanted into the vehicle when he opened the driver's side door. "We're in luck," he said, catching his breath. "We've got a place to stay tonight. Everyone get your slickers on."

Ten minutes later, the four of them reached the front stairs of an old Victorian home. An elderly woman opened the door and waved them in. "You poor things. Come in. Come in. Let's get you warmed up!"

The Calders stepped into the foyer, dripping. "You can hang your slickers on the pegs and come get warm by the fire," the woman offered, motioning to the hearth in the sitting room. "I'll put some tea on."

"Thank you so much," Ardella said. "You are very kind to let us into your home like this."

"I'm glad for the company. I'll get the tea going and then we can get acquainted."

Ardella, Randolph and the boys gathered around the fireplace. How good it felt to be out of the elements with a roof overhead.

Five minutes later, the woman returned with a tray containing a tea pot, five mugs, a bowl of honey, and a plate of molasses cookies. She set it down on a walnut coffee table and poured hot tea into the mugs. Looking at the boys, she said, "Help yourselves to some cookies. These were my boy's favorite."

The boys looked at their mother. She nodded. "What do you say?"

"Thank you," the boys said in unison, reaching for the cookies.

The old lady smiled. "You two are quite welcome." Then she glanced over at Ardella. "How far along are you?"

Ardella rubbed her stomach. "About eight months."

"Well, I suspect you're quite anxious to get where it is you're headed."

"That we are," Randolph said. "San Diego, California is our destination."

"Randolph's cousin works in a garage there," Ardella put in. "Randolph has a job waiting."

Randolph nodded. "It's just part-time, but it's something. There sure isn't any work back home."

"Where is home?" the woman inquired.

"Hampton Roads,Virginia."

It turned out the woman had once been there with her husband, had thought highly of the community. For the next hour, the five of them stayed by the fireplace in the sitting room getting acquainted. The boys played checkers and ate molasses cookies while the adults talked.

The woman's name was Maria Giordana. She and her parents had moved to America when she was a girl. They settled in Boston. Maria was just seventeen when she met Mario Giordana. They moved to Oklahoma where Mario found work in the oil industry.

The boys yawned. "Well," declared Maria, "I suppose you are all in need of some rest after your journey. This is the warmest room in the house, you'll be best off here. I'll get some linens and blankets."

"Let me give you a hand," Ardella offered.

Randolph stood. "You stay and rest, sweetheart. I'll help."

A half hour later the Calder family was asleep on the sitting room floor, lying on a feather comforter under blankets, before a glowing fireplace. A scene fit for a Norman Rockwell painting.

The smell of bacon and pancakes wafted in from the kitchen when Ardella woke the following morning. The boys were still fast asleep. She heard laughter coming from the kitchen. Randolph's baritone voice. And Maria's too. They seemed to be enjoying each other's company. Their mood was a sharp contrast to the weather outside.

A glance out the room's only window revealed dark skies, wind, and slanting rain. The driveway was now a muddy river. Ardella pulled the blankets up to her chin and closed her eyes for a few more winks of much needed sleep. But then she bolted upright. The comforter underneath her was wet…her water broke.

Randolph ran to the room at her call, Mrs. Giordana just behind him. Randolph's eyes were panic stricken, but Mrs. Giordana was steady as you please. "Let's get you up, honey," she said. "My bed is just down the hall. I put fresh linens on this morning—just in case."

"Do you have a car?" Randolph asked the woman.

"No, but the doctor does," she said, reading his mind. "He can come to us. This won't be the first baby delivered in this house. Most babies here about are home-delivered. The hospital is two counties away."

They were at the entrance to the bedroom now. "You stay with your wife, I'll call the doctor," Maria instructed.

Ardella slowly made her way to the bed with Randolph's help. The wind was howling outside; rain pelted the side of the house. They listened intently as Mrs. Giordana picked up the phone in the next room and made the call…The woman gasped.

"Oh lord, the phone wires are down."

Ardella winced. The contractions had started.

"How far away is the doctor's office?" Randolph asked.

"Too far to walk. About twenty miles. But the good news is there is a midwife nearby, Mrs. Smith. She delivered many a baby hereabouts before the doctor started his practice."

There was a frantic look in Randolph's eyes. "How far?"

"The Smith's live about four miles down the road."

"They have a car?"

"No. But they have a tractor."

"Which direction?"

"West. Take a right at the end of the driveway and keep going till you see a white clapboard house on the right. You'll see the name on their mailbox at the edge of the road."

Randolph looked into his wife's eyes. "I love you. I'll be back soon."

“Be careful, love.” Ardella winced as another contraction hit, the lines on her face deeper now.

Randolph bolted from the room and donned his slicker on the way out of the house.

“Can we come?” Randolph Jr. asked.

“Not this time, son. You boys be good.”

*****

There was a grandfather clock in the bedroom. Ardella thought time had never moved slower. She glanced at the clock off and on. The boys, bless their hearts, were content playing a marathon round of checkers in the sitting room.

“Don’t you worry about a thing,” Mrs. Giordana told Ardella. “The Lord is watching over us. Mrs. Smith has delivered many a baby in her day, and she’ll be arriving at any moment.”

An hour passed. Then another. And yet another. The old woman remained at Ardella’s side, wiping her brow with damp towels.

Then, with the contractions just a minute apart, there was a ruckus at the front of the house. A moment later, Mrs. Smith stepped into the room, followed by Randolph. He was limping. Later, Randolph would recall the story of his journey: how he fell and twisted his ankle in a pothole; the look on the Smith’s faces when he knocked on their door; the return trip on the tractor.

"How you doin' there, honey?" Mrs. Smith asked, opening her bag. She was a heavyset older woman with hooped silver rings in each ear. She was an angel, Ardella thought. And then came another contraction, the sharpest pain yet. It was nearly unbearable.

"Okay husband," the woman said to Randolph. "You've done your job. You best stay with your boys out in the sittin' room now. They're needin' their daddy. We got work to do."

Randolph limped over to the bed and kissed Ardella.

"Go now. Shoo!"

"Yes ma'am."

An hour later came the wail of a newborn baby. Mrs. Smith stepped into the sitting room and wiped her brow.

"Congratulations, Mr. Calder. Your daughter is beautiful."

Ardella slowly gained her strength back in the days that followed. She lingered in bed with baby Isabella and took slow walks around the house. Randolph's ankle was on the mend. He used a makeshift crutch for a few days, and his limp was a little less noticeable each day.

Never one to sit idle long, Randolph was soon up to his old self, fiddling around with things. He replaced broken sash cords, replaced some rotted porch boards and repaired leaky faucets using tools he found out back in Mrs.Giordana's husband's tool shed. "Make yourself at home out there," the kindly woman told him. "Use what you like, take what you need. Nobody else will be using that stuff. My Mario, God rest his soul, would be glad to know his beloved tools are being put to use. Lord only knows how many hours he spent out there in that shed tinkering with this and that."

Inside the shed, a workbench lined the far wall, complete with a vise and small anvil. And there was a small woodstove in the corner. Lightly rusted hand tools lined the surface of the work-bench: claw hammers, pliers, tin snips, nail sets, a hand drill, various wrenches, and a hatchet, all neatly arranged. There were jars of screws, small paper bags of nails, piles of sheet metal, an old kerosene blowtorch, and even a roll of welding solder. And there were cans of paint, too. Mario Giordana had indeed been a tinkerer.

It was the sheet metal that caught Randolph's interest. He managed to get the Ford up the driveway and pulled it up to the shed. Then he cut a square from a section of sheet metal and welded it over the hole in the radiator with the kerosene blowtorch. Mission accomplished.

Mrs. Giordana encouraged the Calders to stay as long as they wished. "At least through Christmas," she said. "You must stay for *Christmas*." With so much going on in their lives, they hadn't given much thought to the holidays. It was already December 23rd.

"Children deserve to be in a warm home at Christmas," Mrs. Giordana went on. "You folks owe it to yourselves, too."

Ardella and Randolph knew the woman was right. And with young Isabella nursing, delaying their trip a few more days was an attractive thought. It was a fine offer. "On one condition," Ardella said.

"Oh, what's that?"

"We help out with the cooking. And the decorating and chores."

Mrs. Giordana gestured with her hand. "You just rest up and tend to little Isabella there. I'll take care of the cooking. It will be my honor. Randolph here has already done more than enough work around this old place. We could do with a Christmas tree, though," she said, looking at Randolph. "There's a strip of woodland out back, about a half mile behind the house. My Mario always found a good tree there."

Randolph grinned. "Boys, get your jackets."

The three of them returned an hour later proudly dragging a Scotch pine. Randolph cut two boards for a base and nailed them to the end of the trunk in an x pattern.

"Oh my," Mrs. Giordana exclaimed when they brought the tree inside. "Let's get it set up in the sitting room. Then you boys can help me make some Christmas cookies. How would that be?"

"Cookies! Great!" the boys shouted.

Metal cookie cutters were laid out on the counter, along side a bowl of cookie dough when Randolph Jr. and Jimmy padded into the kitchen. There were bells, candy canes, a snowman, a

Christmas tree, stockings and a gingerbread man.

That evening, the boys proudly carried a tray of cookies to their parents and Isabella in the sitting room. "Why thanks, boys!" Randolph boomed. The man was known for his sweet tooth. "And to you, Maria."

Mrs. Giordana blushed. "My pleasure. It's not every day I'm blessed with such fine company as these two. How they remind me of my boy at their age."

Randolph placed a log in the fireplace and they all settled back, absorbing the warmth. Then Jimmy spoke up. "There's no decorations on the tree. We need to decorate it."

Mrs. Giordana grew silent for a moment. "I'm afraid I don't have any decorations," she said finally. "I did have some, a bunch in fact. They were stored in the attic…The roof leaked last year and I lost them all."

"The tree is a gift in itself, boys," Ardella said. "And that wonderful pine scent. Can you smell it?"

The boys sniffed. Yes, they thought so too…But still, the tree did seem odd without decorations. Randolph bit into a cookie. And an idea came to him.

The next morning, Christmas Eve, found Randolph and the boys in the tool shed. A fire crackled in the woodstove as Randolph laid a sheet of tin on the workbench. He then handed cookie cutters to the boys and instructed them to trace patterns on the sheet of tin.

After that, Randolph instructed the boys in the art of using tin snips. They watched as their father cut out the shapes, one-by-one. There were a dozen in all. When the last shape was cut out, they placed them on the workbench. There were bells, candy canes, snowmen, Christmas trees, stockings and a gingerbread man.

Randolph picked up a hammer and nail and tapped a hole into the top of each ornament. Next he cut small pieces of wire and instructed the boys on how to fashion them into hooks. When the boys were finished crafting hooks, their father opened the paints: red, silver, green and gold. The boys set about painting the ornaments. They had great fun. They finished just before noon and decided to surprise the women back at the house.

"What have you fellas been up to?" Ardella asked when they returned.

"Oh, nothing much," Randolph smiled. "Just puttering around."

"Yeah," little Jimmy beamed. "We were just puttering around."

Randolph Jr. joined in. "That's right Mom. Puttering."

They waited until the two women were out of the room. Then Randolph and the boys hung the ornaments on the tree. Afterward they called Ardella, Isabella, and Mrs. Gioradana into the room.

"Oh my, now *that* is a Christmas tree," said Mrs. Giordana.

"It's just beautiful," exclaimed Ardella, hugging the boys.

Isabella stared at the ornaments in wonderment.

After lunch, Randolph summoned the boys. "Let's go."

"Where?" Jimmy asked.

Randolph bent down and whispered into the boy's ear. "Back to the shed."

The tool shed was now the boys' favorite place. They eagerly followed their father. Inside the shed, Randolph stoked the coals in the woodstove and mounded them in a pile with an iron pole. Then he wedged the tip of his soldering iron into the coals and left it there. The boys watched curiously.

Next, Randolph selected a sheet of tin from the scrap pile. This metal was thicker than the metal they had used for the ornaments. The boys watched as their father worked the tin snips to cut two squares from the sheet.

"What are we making Dad?"

"You'll soon see."

Randolph placed the squares of metal on the work bench. Then, using a ruler and pencil, he drew horizontal lines on each sheet and made precision cuts along the lines with the tin snips. The boys watched in awe as their father crafted the metal into two rectangular tins and soldered the corner joints.

Once this was completed, Randolph repeated the process and crafted lids for the tins. When he finished, he placed a lid on the first tin and gently pushed down. It was a snug fit. The same was true of the second one. They were as good as any store-bought tins.

"Okay boys, you can paint `em now."

Jimmy furrowed his brow. "You mean paint them like the ornaments?"

"Anything you want."

"Holly," Randolph Jr. said.

"Huh?" This from Jimmy.

"Holly leaves," Randolph Jr. clarified. "Remember Mom telling us about the holly on the farm where she grew up?"

"Fine idea," his father commented.

"There should be berries too," said Jimmy. "Holly berries. They're red."

"Another fine idea," their father remarked.

And so, the boys set to work painting holly leaves and berries on the first tin. They were so pleased with their work that they painted the second tin in the same fashion.

The boys could hardly contain their excitement on Christmas morning. As usual they woke first. To their credit, they remained quiet, not disturbing their parents. It seemed like hours passed. Then Isabella cried out ever so softly. It was just enough to wake their parents. And Mrs. Giordana too.

Way to go Isabella. The boys were quite pleased with their little sister. She was going to be all right. Soon everyone was gathered around the tree.

Underneath the tree were two presents of equal size. Each was wrapped in brown paper—cut from paper bags. Randolph and the boys had wrapped the presents in the shed the night before.

MERRY CHRISTMAS was painted on the top of each present in bold red letters. The boys handed one of the presents to their mother.

Ardella smiled. "I had a feeling you boys were up to something." Randolph Jr. and Jimmy watched anxiously as their mother unwrapped the gift.

Ardella's eyes grew watery when she saw the Christmas Tin. "It's beautiful. And look at those holly leaves! And the berries! "

"The holly leaves were my idea," Randolph Jr. stated.

"And the berries were my idea," Jimmy chimed in.

Their mother pulled the boys in for a hug. Randolph made his way over for a hug too. "You boys and your father are really something, you know that? I am one lucky lady."

Jimmy glanced over at Mrs. Giordana. "There's one for you too." He handed her the second present.

"Oh my," she said. "You all have already given me so much. Just having you all here has been a gift."

The woman's eyes glistened when she peeled away the paper and saw the Christmas Tin. "Why, it's just like yours, Ardella! Marvelous. Thank you all so very much. This will make for a wonderful reminder of a very special Christmas indeed."

"Uh boys?"

Randolph Jr. and Jimmy looked over at their father.

"Looks like Santa left you something under the tree."

The boys ran to the tree. In the excitement of making and giving gifts, they had not thought about themselves.

Two slingshots lay tucked underneath the tree. They were handcrafted from forked sticks, the slings constructed from rubber inner tubing. And there was a note from St. Nick himself informing the boys how pleased he was with their behavior and help this year. Santa instructed the boys to only use the slingshots in their father's presence until they were older.

"Wow! Can we use them now?"

"I don't see why not," Randolph said. "Let's go."

Randolph had as much fun as the boys, knocking tin cans off the fence rail in the backyard that morning. And when the Smiths stopped by that afternoon with their grandson, they went out again. The Smith's grandson enjoyed the sport of plinking too.

"Tell you what," Randolph told the boy. "If it's okay with your grandfather, I think we may just be able to find some materials around here to make you a slingshot of your own." Mr. Smith nodded and said that would be just fine.

Mrs. Smith brought a fruitcake, the most delicious Ardella had ever tasted. "Old family recipe," the woman confided. "I can write it down if you like."

"I'd like that very much," Ardella said.

It was a fine visit. The three boys played all afternoon, and the Smiths joined them for dinner that night.

The ornaments sparkled in the flickering light from the fireplace as the Calders turned in that night. There would be many more Christmases in the years ahead but never one quite like the Christmas of 1933.

Chapter 18

"That was quite a story," I remarked. Those in the seats around me agreed.

"Glad you enjoyed it. It sure was fun reminiscing. Those were good days, even though money was tight. And I still use that fruitcake recipe to this day."

"Which son are you staying with in Connecticut?" I asked. "Randolph Jr. or Jimmy?"

"Jimmy. He has a family of his own now. I am a proud grandmother."

"How about your other children. Do they live in New England too?"

Ardella's brow furrowed. "No…Randolph Jr. was killed during the war. World War II. My daughter, Isabella, lives in California with her husband. They are both pediatricians."

Just then a nurse poked her head in the room. "Time for dinner, folks."

I stood up to put my coat on. "Thanks for the story," I said to Ardella. "Would you have time for another one Saturday morning?"

Ardella smiled. "You're on."

"Great. Well, see you later and thanks again."

"Thank *you* Jesse. You are the highlight of my day, I'll have you know."

*****

A warm front pushed in from the west and the temperature remained milder than usual for the next several days. It was too warm for pond hockey. By Wednesday, a thin layer of slush layered the pond ice. Skating was taboo. If someone skated on the pond now the ice would be ruined for the season once the next deep freeze set in.

We played street hockey—which was fine by me. After delivering the papers that week, I'd meet up with Larry, Jim and Rob down at the municipal tennis courts and we'd play two vs. two. The town's recreation department had removed the tennis nets at the end of November, and we had the place to ourselves. I played street hockey every day that week but Friday—collection day.

Friday was the longest day on the route, where I had to collect payment from my customers. Some subscribers left their payment in an envelope taped to their door or under a mat. But more often than not, I had to knock on the door and ask for it.

The first three customers left payment envelopes taped to their front door and it appeared I was off to a good start. I deposit-ed the envelopes in my canvas shoulder bag. There was no envelope out at the next customer's house though, the Davis's. I knocked on the door but nobody answered. I knocked again and stood there on the stoop for what seemed a minute or so. I was about to leave when the door opened.

"Hi Jesse," said Mrs. Davis.

"Hello ma'am."

Mrs. Davis handed me an envelope. I thanked her and turned to leave.

"Wait a sec," she said. She reached into her purse and extracted two dollars. She handed me the bills.

"This is for you. Thanks for all of your hard work this year, Jesse."

"Thanks, Mrs. Davis!" I was stunned. I had never received a two dollar tip before. Many customers did not tip at all, and those that did usually just tipped a quarter, maybe fifty cents tops.

"Happy Holidays."

"And to you! Thanks again, Mrs. Davis."

The next customer on the route was Mr.Carhart. He was an old bachelor. The guy was always home and always had his payment check ready. Unlike most customers, he didn't use envelopes. He'd just hand me a check made payable to *The Berkshire Times*. Today was no different. He opened the door as soon as I knocked and handed me a check. I thanked him for his payment. As I stuffed the check in the shoulder bag, he pulled out his wallet and extracted a wrinkled dollar bill. "Fer you," he said, just before he shut the door.

"Thank you," I called out. Another first. The man had never tipped me before. The next customer tipped me $1.75. The one after that, a dollar. The afternoon went on like that. When a customer was home, more often than not, they gave me a tip. It was exhilarating.

I was looking forward to sharing the news with Ardella, but she was eating dinner in the cafeteria with the other patrons by the time I arrived at the nursing home. Ardella had left her payment envelope taped to her front door. I collected it along with the payment envelopes from my other customers at the nursing home. Then I headed home.

The temperature was dropping steadily. The warm spell had come to an end. It was freezing out. I saw my breath in the air, but I didn't feel the cold.

I went straight to my room when I got home and counted the tip revenue. The total was $21.75! I was elated. Being my first year on the route, I hadn't known about Christmas tips. It was a most welcome bonus. When the excitement subsided a little, I began the tedious process of opening the payment envelopes and tabulating the payments.

As a paper boy for *The Berkshire Times*, it was my responsibility to be sure that payment was received from each customer. At the end of the route each Friday, I opened all of the payment envelopes and filled out a "payment sheet," a form that listed all of the addresses on the route. Beside each address were two blank lines, one for the amount of the payment and one for the date. There was also a check box to indicate whether the customer paid by check or cash.

After I filled out the form, I'd enclose it in a green cloth zipper bag, along with all of the payments. Then I'd deposit the bag in a hinged wooden box outside by our front door. The delivery driver, who dropped the bundles of papers off on the front stoop, removed the bag from the box every Saturday morning and exchanged it with an empty one.

The first payment envelope I opened in my room that afternoon contained a note:

THANK YOU FOR A GREAT JOB THIS YEAR. AND FOR NOT THROWING THE PAPER IN THE HEDGES LIKE YOUR PREDECESSOR. KEEP UP THE GREAT WORK!

There was an extra three dollars in the envelope. I thought the customer had overpaid at first...But then it clicked. The extra money was a tip!

The next envelope contained another note:

THANKS FOR THE GREAT SERVICE JESSE.
HAPPY HOLIDAYS!

There was a tip in that envelope too: two dollars. The next envelope was a repeat. A note and a tip. This was getting exciting. Many of the envelopes included a tip. And there were more thank you notes and a few Christmas Cards too. One envelope—from Ardella—contained a five-dollar bill!

In all, there was an additional $21.00 in tip revenue from the envelopes...Which meant I had received a total of $42.75 in tips. Enough to buy a pair of CCM Tacks at Fiske's Department Store! Fiske's was closed at that hour, but I'd go there tomorrow morning as soon as the last paper was delivered. With the drop in the temperature, the ice would be pristine tomorrow—perfect for pond hockey. Things were shaping up. Life was good.

Chapter 19

December 21, 1968

My financial position improved further Saturday morning. Three customers that were not home the day before flagged me down and tipped me when I delivered their paper. I took in another $7.50, bringing my total tips to $50.25. And I had the ten dollars from shoveling the walk at the nursing home. After buying the skates, I would still have enough to buy Mom a gift. Maybe I'd even buy Mr. Beauvier a little something, too.

I moved through the route faster than ever that morning, even with the below-freezing temperatures. As such, I arrived at the nursing home a little earlier than usual.

Ardella was not in her room. I left her paper in the hallway in front of her door. I didn't find her in the sitting room or the cafeteria. I inquired about Ardella at the front desk.

"She's in physical therapy," the nursing coordinator informed me. "Probably be in there a while. They just called her in."

"Thanks."

"You're welcome."

Ardella's next story would have to wait. I had a pair of skates to buy.

After leaving Beldon Manor, I went home to drop off the paper bag and pick up the tip money from my room. The only thing on my mind was those skates…until I saw Mom sitting at the kitchen table, crying.

Mom turned slowly toward me when I stepped into in the kitchen. Her eyes were swollen; her face was puffed out and wet with tears.

"Mom, what's the matter?" I asked, bending down to give her a hug.

It was then that I noticed it. A rectangular-shaped document on the kitchen table. The words Western Union caught my attention. A telegram.

"Oh Jesse," she sobbed quietly, embracing me.

My heart was hammering. Tears welled up in my eyes as I read the telegram:

> THE SECRETARY OF WAR DEEPLY REGRETS TO INFORM YOU THAT YOUR HUSBAND. JACK MACLEAN. SERGEANT. US ARMY IS MISSING FOLLOWING ACTION IN THE PERFORMANCE OF HIS DUTY AND IN THE SERVICE OF HIS COUNTRY.

Chapter 20

Religion didn't play a major a role in our house; we did not attend church on a regular basis. But I prayed that day. A lot.

Dear God. Please watch over Dad and let no harm come to him.

Please God. Protect Dad and keep him safe.

God. I will be forever grateful if you'll help guide my Dad to safety.

Minutes ticked by like hours. Mom and I didn't go out of the house that weekend. I spent most of the time sequestered in my room, my mind constantly on Dad. Mom slowly puttered around the house, cleaning and organizing, lost in worry. I'd never seen her so distraught.

I don't know if Mr. Beauvier was privy to the telegram. But if not, he sensed something was out of kilter. He gave us a wide berth and fixed his own meals.

Later that afternoon, Mom brought me a grilled cheese sandwich and a bowl of chicken soup. She gently placed the meal on my desk. When it was still there hours later, she didn't prod me. Mom didn't have an appetite either.

I didn't sleep Saturday night. I said another round of prayers and laid in bed thinking of Dad, only of him.

Sunday, December 22nd. It was the shortest day of the year according to the calendar on the kitchen wall. But it stretched on forever. Mom called to me from the kitchen that morning. She made us toast and scrambled eggs. "You've got to eat. At least a little," she said.

I still had no appetite but managed to eat a piece of toast and some of the eggs. Then I retreated to my room for the day. Around seven o'clock that night there was a knock on my door. I got up and opened the door. Mr. Beauvier stood in the hallway. This was a first.

"The Bruins are playing the Canadiens tonight… Game will be on soon."

"I know," I mumbled.

I didn't make it to the living room to watch the game with Mr. Beauvier that night.

Monday morning. Mom called a co-worker to cover her shift at the hospital. Then she came to my room. I was still in bed.

"Get ready for school honey," she said, gently tousling my hair.

I sighed. "It's just an early release day. School lets out at noon for Christmas break. We're not going to learn anything." Going to school was the last thing I felt like doing. I didn't want to talk to friends, and I didn't want to deal with teachers.

"It will do you good to get out of the house for a while."

I left for school later than usual to avoid walking with my friends. I didn't want to talk to *anyone*. It was too painful. But people somehow knew, perhaps from my mother's call to the hospital that morning. Some kids at school had parents and other relatives that worked at the hospital.

I looked down as I walked the school hallways that morning, avoiding eye contact. A lot of guys were talking about Boston's 7-5 win against Montreal. Larry tracked me down in the hallway later that morning. "Hey Jesse. I'm so sorry, man. I heard about your father."

The tears welled in my eyes instantly. I couldn't talk. It was all I could do to nod my head and walk away.

I didn't share in my classmate's jubilation when the dismissal bell rang at noon, signaling the start of Christmas break. I took a different route home that day to avoid having to talk with my friends. The route eventually cut along the east end of the pond. The ice was pristine. Larry and the guys would no doubt be out there that afternoon. But hockey was the furthest thing from my mind.

Chapter 21

The stack of papers was in the usual place when I got home. There was no avoiding the paper route. "The papers have to be delivered no matter what, in all conditions: rain, snow, hail or sleet," the route manager told me when I took over the route. He hadn't mentioned anything about grief or despair.

I delivered the papers in slow motion, taking twice as long as usual to deliver each paper. But I didn't care. The customers were receiving their papers, they had no complaint.

It was three o'clock when I reached Beldon Manor. I passed by the sitting room without glancing over at the Christmas tree. Christmas was far removed from my thoughts.

I was planning to leave Ardella's paper in the hallway, just outside her room, but her door was open. She spotted me right away; there was no escaping her. The woman knew something was wrong the second she saw me. "Oh Jesse dear, what's wrong?"

Tears streamed down my cheeks. I tried to talk but instead broke down and began to cry. Ardella embraced me in a hug.

"Come in," she said softly. "Come in and sit down."

Ardella closed the door and guided me to a small chair. I sat down. She pulled up another chair and sat across from me. I continued to cry, sobbing without control now. She patted me on the shoulder and sat there silently as I wailed.

I must have cried for a full ten minutes, maybe more. Finally, I looked over at Ardella.

"...My...f-father... he's...MIA...Missing-In-Action."

"*Oh Jesse*, I'm *so* sorry to hear that."

She was the only person I had opened up to about it. Over the next five minutes I filled her in on the details, informed her about the telegram. Told her what we knew. Ardella listened attentively. She was a great listener.

After I filled her in, a few moments passed in silence. Ardella's eyes were fixed on the window across the room. Eventually, I turned to glance out the window to see what it was that had captured Ardella's attention outside the window.

When I looked, I realized that she was not looking out the window, but rather at the object resting on the windowsill. The Christmas Tin.

Ardella stood and made her way over to the tin. She picked it up and carried it back to her chair. Then she sat down and placed the tin on her lap. She sat there for a while, as if her mind was wrestling with something. The silence was comforting in a way. I said nothing, nor did she.

A few more minutes passed. Then Ardella broke the silence.

"...One thing I have learned over the years," she began, "is *faith*. You're dealing with something that no boy should ever have to experience, something no family should ever have to experience. I won't say that I know what you're feeling or what you're going through right now. But I can tell you that *faith* has helped me deal with some tragic situations in my life over the years."

"Faith?" I asked, wiping away my tears.

Ardella nodded. "Yes, having faith. Webster's may have a slightly different definition, but to me, faith is believing in something and maintaining hope. Having confidence in a positive outcome."

Easy for you to say.

Ardella removed the lid from the Christmas Tin. Then she slowly extracted a folded document from the tin. She opened it gently and smoothed the creases. From the discoloration around the edges, I could tell it was old.

"I hadn't planned to show you this. Or to tell you about it. And I'm a bit hesitant still. I've struggled with the decision to show it to you, in fact. But a bigger part of me feels it's beneficial to share this with you now. Please forgive me if you don't feel the same. My intention may seem questionable at first when you read it".

Ardella handed me the document. I immediately recognized two words in bold print at the top: WESTERN UNION. A telegram. The telegram was similar in size to the one we received notifying us about Dad. But this one referred to Randolph Calder, Gunner's Mate. And it was from the Navy Department. I read the first sentence:

THE NAVY DEPARTMENT DEEPLY REGRETS TO

INFORM YOU THAT YOUR HUSBAND RANDOLPH CALDER GUNNER'S MATE FIRST CLASS USN WAS KILLED IN ACTION IN THE PERFORMANCE OF HIS DUTY AND IN THE SERVICE TO HIS COUNTRY.

Why show me this?

I looked over at Ardella.

"My husband, Randolph, volunteered for the Navy when America entered the war," she said. "He was assigned to the USS Jacob Jones, a destroyer. It was torpedoed by a German submarine. Sixty-six men were lost."

I was at a complete loss as to why she was telling me a-bout this. Was it to show me that she was from a military family too? That she had lost someone dear to her? I was befuddled. "My grandfather fought in World War II too," I said. It was the only thing that came to mind for a reply.

"This wasn't World War II," Ardella remarked. "Randolph served during the First World War. Look at the postmark."

I glanced at the telegram. It was dated December 1917. Now I was confused. The third story she had told me, the one a-bout her and her husband, Randolph, and the boys staying with Mrs. Giordana took place in the 1930's. How could that be if Randolph didn't make it through World War I?

"I don't understand," I said. "Your husband, Randolph, died in World War I. In 1917. Did you make up the story about your family staying with Mrs. Giordana during the Depression? Or, did you marry again, to another man named Randolph?"

Ardella shook her head no. "Neither."

"Huh?"

"The telegram was incorrect. It was a mistake. Randolph was rescued when the ship went down. He made it through the war safely. He just passed on a few years ago."

"…I see."

"Not everything is as it seems," Ardella said, looking into my eyes. "*Faith,* Jesse. Have faith, dear boy, it will guide you through this troubling time."

I thought about Ardella's words on the way home. But I was too overwhelmed with grief to comprehend them.

Chapter 22

December 24, 1968

It was snowing when the papers arrived the next day, Christmas Eve. The roads were slick—too slick for a bike. I delivered the papers on foot that morning. There was slush on the road and my boots were soon saturated. It was slow going.

As I trudged along, I reflected back to the visit with Ardella the previous afternoon. *Faith*. I tried to be hopeful—the telegram said Dad was *missing*. It did not mention the other word. Still…I couldn't help but worry about the possibility of the other scenario. It was all too probable. Dad was in my every thought. And I knew it was the same for Mom.

Ardella was with her doctor when I arrived at the nursing home. I would not see her that day. After delivering the papers to my customers at Beldon Manor, I zipped up my jacket and headed outside for the trek home. My clothing was wet and my feet were going numb. I was freezing.

My teeth were chattering by the time I got home; I was chilled. But when I saw Mom on the phone in kitchen, I suddenly wasn't cold anymore. She was crying…But she was not distraught. Mom was smiling, in fact. The tears running down her cheeks were from joy. When she saw me, she handed me the phone. "It's your father."

"Dad?!"

Through the static, I heard: "Jesse! It's me, son. I'm okay."

"My God Dad! You're okay?" Now I was crying too.

"Never been better."

"What happened?"

"Long story short—three of us were captured but we managed to escape. Made it back to our unit with just a few scratches and a sprain. I'll tell you all about it when I get home next year."

"Thank *God,* Dad!"

"What's all this talk about God?"

I smiled. "I've been doing a lot of praying lately."

"Well, that's a good thing. I think it worked. Hey, like I said in my letters, thanks for stepping up and taking care of things while I'm over here."

"No sweat, Dad. Where are you now?"

"The CO moved us to the rear for a few days of R&R. So don't worry about your Dad. I'm safe as can be. We have hot chow. And there's a PX— a store that sells cold Coke's and anything else we need. It's been a gift."

"Sounds great Dad."

"Listen sport, I wish I could talk longer but I've got to go. There's a line of guys waiting for the phone. There are lines for everything in the military. I won't miss them."

"I love you, Dad."

"I love you too, Jess. Take care of Mom and have a good Christmas."

I ran over to Mom and we embraced each other. For a long time. When we finally let go of one another, Mom wiped away her tears and said, "We have a tree to decorate."

"And cookies to bake," I added. Mom and I always made a batch of Christmas cookies on Christmas Eve.

"How about a little lunch first?"

I suddenly realized I was very hungry. My appetite had returned with a vengeance. "Grilled cheese and bacon?"

"You bet."

I extracted the box of Christmas decorations from the hallway closet and unwound the lights while Mom prepared lunch. After lunch, we spent the afternoon decorating the tree and making sugar cookies.

It was a little past four o'clock when it hit me. *Presents*. I had yet to buy one for Mom. "I'll be back in a little while," I called out.

"Okay, honey."

I made it to Fiske's Department Store twenty minutes before they closed. Just enough time to find a gift for Mom, or so I hoped. I went straight to the women's department. On the way to the store, I had developed a list of possibilities: a woolen hat, a scarf, a pair of gloves. Maybe a holiday sweater.

I looked at the items on the shelves as I walked down the aisles in the women's department. Then I came to the display area…and saw the red Christmas dress. The one Mom had been admiring.

I glanced at the price tag. I had not planned on spending that kind of money. Buying the dress would mean no skates. I didn't have money for both.

After selecting Mom's gift, as an afterthought, I made my way over to the hardware section. There, I picked up a compact toolkit for Mr. Beauvier. It would fit neatly in the glove compartment of his sedan.

On the walk home, I could see Beldon Manor illuminated in the distance. And I immediately thought of Ardella, couldn't wait to tell her the news about Dad. I arrived at the nursing home five minutes later.

There was nobody at the front desk. I made my way down the hall. The Christmas tree in the sitting room was majestic, all lit up and adorned with tinsel and ornaments. Several residents were gathered in front it, watching *It's A Wonderful Life* on the Zenith.

The door to Ardella's room was open when I arrived… All of her possessions were gone. The holiday afghan. The pressed clothes in the closet. The candles she never lit. The Christmas Tin. There was no sign of Ardella's presence at all; it was as if she had never been there.

A nurse came down the hall and stopped when she saw me in front of Room 12. "She moved out this morning," the

the woman informed me.

"Moved out?"

"Yes, mentioned something about moving to Connecticut to be with family."

"...Thanks." With everything going on, I completely forgot about Ardella's plans to move to Connecticut. The thought that I would never see her again hadn't crossed my mind.

"Merry Christmas," the nurse smiled.

"Merry Christmas."

Chapter 23

Christmas

I woke to the aroma of apples and cinnamon. Mom had a pot of hot cider on the stove, another Maclean family holiday tradition. She was sitting on the couch admiring the Christmas tree, sipping a mug of cider when I padded into the living room. I had never seen her more at peace and relaxed.

"Merry Christmas, kiddo."

"Merry Christmas, Mom." I took a seat beside her on the couch and she tousled my hair.

Beneath the tree were two presents. One was the gift for Mom, which I had wrapped the night before. The other was a mystery.

"I have a gift for you," I announced. I picked the gift up from under the tree and handed it to her.

"Oh Jesse. Thanks sweetheart. You are *something*."

Mom took great care in opening gifts; she went to great lengths to avoid ripping wrapping paper. And today was no exception. She carefully removed the tape from the wrapping at one end and carefully pulled the box out.

Her eyes grew watery as she opened the box. "Oh Jesse. It's beautiful!" My mother removed the Christmas dress from the box and held it up. A few moments passed as she admired the dress. It was so good to see her smile. That was a gift in itself.

Mom gently placed the dress on the couch and hugged me, her tears wet against my cheek. "Thank you honey. Thank you *so* much. This is the nicest gift I have ever received."

"Merry Christmas, Mom."

"Merry Christmas!"

Mom got up and made her way over to the tree. She picked up the other present—a neatly wrapped box, bound with red ribbon. She handed it to me.

"For you."

I didn't waste any time unwrapping the box. Inside it was a pair of Cooper hockey gloves. "Thanks, Mom!"

"You're welcome sport."

My old gloves were shot. The leather palms were worn through. I'd never owned a new pair of hockey gloves, always bought them used at the thrift store. I would get a lot of use out the gloves…next year. I still hadn't told Mom that my skates no longer fit.

"Where's Mr. Beauvier this morning?" I inquired. I was anxious to show him the gloves.

"Visiting his daughter."

"He has a daughter?"

"Yes, she lives in Albany. Mr. Beauvier left yesterday when you were delivering papers."

"Oh."

"He left something for you," Mom said.

She got up, went to the kitchen, and returned with a box-shaped gift wrapped in newspaper. She handed it to me. "Let's see what Mr. Beauvier got you."

I was curious about the gift. It was too heavy to be clothes. I removed the paper—and my heart raced when I read the wording on the box: CCM Tacks. Size 8.

I sat there awestruck for a few seconds. Then I opened the box and removed the skates. Mom whistled.

"That's some gift!"

"Yes it is," I grinned. Hockey season was shaping up.

Mom seemed to read my mind. "Okay, let's get you some breakfast. Then you can go to the pond."

After a sportsman's breakfast of pancakes, bacon, home fries and juice, I spent the rest of the morning and the whole afternoon at the pond. For the first hour it was just me. Then, Larry, Jim and Rob arrived. We played hockey for hours. It was exhilarating. Darkness was setting in when we finally quit.

When I got home, a white van was pulling away from the curb. A sign on the vehicle's side door read *Beldon Catering*. I had seen their vans around town, but never in our neighborhood.

When I stepped into the house the aroma of turkey wafted in from the kitchen. On the kitchen table rested a roast turkey on a platter. Surrounding it were assorted dishes: green beans, stuffing, mashed potatoes, cranberry sauce, and a salad. And there was a large basket of crescent rolls. The day just kept getting better.

"Where did all *this* come from?" I asked.

"Do you know an…Ardella?" Mom asked.

"Yes. She is—was, one of my customers."

Mom handed me a Christmas card. "It was delivered with the meal."

It was a simple card. On the front cover was a print of an old faded white cottage with a wreath on the front door. There was writing on the reverse side:

Merry Christmas and Happy Holidays.

Best Wishes,

Ardella

P.S. Jesse, this cottage is a lot like the one on the farm in Virginia.

.

I hadn't had a bite to eat since that morning. I was famished after playing hockey all day. Mom and I loaded our plates and ate in front of the television. The Bruins were playing the Seals, and we watched the game as we ate. We finished dinner just as the first period ended.

Mom took our plates to the kitchen and returned a minute later. "I know you've already given me the most wonderful gift a son ever gave his mother, but I'd like to ask you for one more gift."

I looked at Mom quizzically. "Yes?"

"Be right back."

It was nighttime now. The living room lights were off; the lights on the Christmas tree provided the only illumination in the room.

Mom went down the hall and stepped into her room. She returned a few minutes later. She was wearing the Christmas dress. Mom looked radiant.

Bing Crosby's *White Christmas* emanated from the stereo: *I'm dreaming of a White Christmas....*

"Would you gift me with a dance?" Mom asked.

"I'd be honored."

We danced in front of the Christmas tree, and all was right in the world.

Epilogue

December 24, 2000

Dusk was settling in. It was still snowing with no sign of letting up; the logs in the fireplace had diminished to coals. I glanced over at Anna. She was looking at the Christmas Tin.

"Did you ever see Ardella again?" she asked.

"No. Ardella never returned to Beldon."

"...Well, then how did the Christmas Tin become yours? I don't remember you saying that she gave it to you." My daughter was always thinking.

"You were really paying attention there, kiddo. I didn't mention that part, did I? About how I received the Christmas Tin."

"No."

"About four years after Ardella left, when I was in high school, an attorney called the house. It was December. I remember I had just come home from hockey practice. The man informed me that Ardella had passed away. He said her family was with her at the time and that she had passed peacefully, without pain.

The lawyer informed me that Ardella's will included a list of her personal property and that she had designated beneficiaries for each item in her will. He said the Christmas Tin was included on the list, and he informed me that Ardella had bequeathed it to me. He had called to get my address. The Christmas Tin arrived in the mail about a week later."

"Can I open the Christmas Tin now?" Anna asked.

"Absolutely."

Anna lifted the Christmas Tin from the coffee table. Then she gently removed the lid and peered inside.

She removed the items inside one at a time, starting with Ardella's gifts and mementos—the turtle dove, the brittle corn husk ornament, the telegram. Then she removed the things I had placed in the tin over the years: a 1969 picture of Mom, Dad and me in front of a Christmas tree; a 1970 ticket stub from a Christmas Day Bruins game (a gift from Dad); a homemade tinfoil star from the year my wife and I married; an old handcrafted ornament my grandfather had provided; a cardboard cut-out ornament Anna made in nursery school; a picture of Anna and Paul with Santa.

"We need to put something in the tin from this Christmas," Anna stated.

"Great idea."

"What though?"

"Well, Christmas isn't until tomorrow. We've got some time. I'm sure you'll think of something—"

"Grandma! Grandpa!" Paul shouted from the next room. Mom and Dad had just pulled into the driveway.

Anna ran out to greet her grandparents. I got up and added a few logs to the fireplace. Then I turned on the hi-fi and tuned it to a station playing Christmas music. When I turned around, Mom was standing there admiring the tree.

She was wearing a holiday outfit, a red blouse and dark slacks. The years had been kind to her. She was as beautiful as ever. Mom met me halfway across the room and we hugged.

"Merry Christmas, Mom."

"Merry Christmas, sweetheart."

Dad entered the room a few minutes later. The years had been kind to him as well. He stood there healthy as can be, his silver hair still cut military-style, his back ramrod straight. Paul was at his side, tugging on his hand.

"Grandpa, come have a Christmas cookie."

Dad smiled and gave us a nod as he headed off in tow to the kitchen.

As Mom and I stood there talking, Anna sneaked up with her Polaroid and snapped a picture. She handed the picture to me. Mom and I were perfectly centered in front of the tree. "For the Christmas Tin," she said.

"You don't want to wait until tomorrow to choose something for the Christmas Tin?" I asked.

Anna smiled. "This is just the first picture. I have a lot more film. Can we put *more* than one thing in the Christmas Tin this year?"

"I don't see why not. You bet."

Anna left the room to take more pictures. And so began a new Maclean family holiday tradition.

Just then, the opening lyrics of Bing Crosby's *White Christmas* emanated from the hi-fi. I held my hand out to Mom.

"Would you care for a dance?"

"Love to."

We danced in front of the Christmas tree. And for a moment, it was December 1968, and all was right in the world.

Made in the USA
Lexington, KY
26 November 2016